FIVE THINGS I

love

ABOUT YOU

A CHASE BROTHERS STORY

SARAH
BALLANCE

Entangled Publishing, LLC
2614 South Timberline Road
Suite 109
Fort Collins, CO 80525
Visit our website at www.entangledpublishing.com.

Lovestruck is an imprint of Entangled Publishing, LLC.

Edited by Tracy Montoya and Heather Howland
Cover design by Heather Howland
Cover art by iStock

Manufactured in the United States of America

First Edition August 2015

For anyone who has ever rattled a fire escape.

Chapter One

Grocery store road rage.

It was a definite thing.

Estelle Donovan bit back a rather indelicate bout of profanity and made a silent vow not to earn a spot on the evening news before she made it out of the produce section. Unfortunately, that was in the hands of the very angry man who, after causing a collision with her shopping cart, had just dropped what had to be ten pounds of loose pistachios on the shiny, waxed floor. The nuts had hit the ground running, and she briefly wondered if she should follow suit. But despite the general discontent of pretty much everyone she'd encountered in this urban hell, she couldn't bear to be that... impolite.

She stared at the red-faced elderly gent and wondered if he had an ounce of agility left. If so, she was screwed. "I'm sorry about your...nuts," she sputtered. "Really sorry."

"Beat it, lady."

No need to tell her twice. Her survival instincts took over, and she put it in reverse to make her escape, wincing as shells crunched underfoot. Once clear of the ransacked display of loose nuts, she spun her cart to face the opposite direction, only to nearly take out a towering stack of Spaghetti-Os. What were they doing in the freaking produce section? BLOWOUT SALE, the sign read. *Mmkay*. Putting them on sale did not make them produce. They belonged down one of those teeny, narrow aisles, crammed together like pretty much everything else in the land of asphalt and concrete.

She. Hated. Cities.

Her brother was off at some tech writer conference, and Estelle was spending her vacation at his place in New York City, thousands of miles from her west coast home. While her responsibilities withered in the California warmth without her, she was stuck babysitting a dreary apartment the size of a shoe box. One not stocked with the groceries Grady had promised. Not unless a half-full Chinese takeout container and half-empty bottle of ketchup qualified as "stocked" in these parts. And even if they did...they didn't.

Estelle pulled up the list she'd made on her cell phone. She could have saved a lot of time and just written "everything," but then she'd forget something essential. Something like jalapeños. Those were non-negotiable. She used pickled jalapeños like most people used salt or ketchup. Determined not to forget them, she made a beeline for the condiment aisle...which was blocked. While she waited for a woman with two screaming toddlers to maneuver out of the way, she consulted her list. It was a mile long.

Definitely *everything*.

One of the kids had a death grip on a now-misshapen box of sugar packaged as cereal. The kid's reaction to his mother's attempts to part him from it redefined "bloody murder," and not one passerby raised a brow over the screams, which *really* had Estelle re-thinking her promise to live here, even temporarily.

She found an aisle that wasn't completely clogged with shoppers and took it, grabbing stuff from the shelves as she went. She no longer cared if she spent a fortune or if her ingredients would even come together into something palatable. She just wanted to get out of there with food, and enough of it that she wouldn't have to come back any time soon. A bargain bin of toothpaste near some canned goods had her thinking there needed to be a federal law that all grocery stores employ the same layout. This place made no sense.

She paused at the end of the detour aisle, wondering if the store sold wine. And if so, if she could drink it while waiting to check out. When Grady had asked her to apartment-sit for him, two weeks hadn't sounded so bad. But that was before she'd found herself in a world of godawful concrete slabs bathed in the stench of sewage. All around her, skyscrapers closed in like giant, menacing walls. She had no idea how her brother could live in such an impersonal place. Not only was the city ugly and devoid of living greenery, but no one, absolutely no one, smiled. If anyone was happy to be there, they hid it well.

She found the pickle aisle but not the jalapeños. After an interminable search, serenaded by the screaming cereal kid parked one aisle over, she spied them on the bottom shelf. Perhaps the day could be saved after all. She knelt down in front of her shopping cart and touched heaven.

Then something exploded overhead.

She ducked, for what good it did, because explosions had a way of triggering that instinct in a person. Then she realized the source of the noise. The corner of her shopping cart had inexplicably rammed the upper shelf of pickle jars, sending several crashing to the floor in a smattering of broken glass and mutated cucumbers. And as she crouched there, clutching her hard-won jalapeños, she realized to her dismay that the front of her white T-shirt was soaked in pickle juice. *Cold* pickle juice.

She *really* should have worn a bra.

"Are you okay?"

She looked toward the sound of the voice, and, to her horror, found it belonged to absolute hotness. The man was utter devastation in well-worn jeans and a shirt that looked like it would have to be clawed off. Not that it was tight, but rather it fell against him *just so* to make no secret of the fact that dude was *ripped*. His biceps made a joke of his shirt-sleeves, and despite the way he leaned over her, his abs remained resolutely flat against what she could see of his waistband beneath the fabric. His jaw, requisitely square, hosted just enough stubble to promise delirium-inducing friction, which was beyond okay because sensual lips promised to soothe every ache.

He also had the greenest eyes she'd ever seen. Positively electric in their intensity, they focused on her.

Her and her pickle-juiced nipples.

Old man nutsack would just love this.

Tall-blond-and-tousled reached for her. When he touched her hand, he set off an explosion that she could practically see reflecting in his green eyes. "I'm sorry," he said. "I didn't see you down there…um, under your shopping cart."

She let him help her to her feet, still struck mute by his ridiculously good looks. He seemed vaguely familiar, although considering how recently she'd arrived in the city, and her general avoidance of eye contact with strangers, she couldn't imagine from where.

"So…you're okay?" His expression suggested he'd already formed an opinion on that particular topic, but if he had, he let it go. Probably safer that way.

"Fine. Just…chilly." Brilliant. The response just screamed *look at my nipples*. And of course he did. Long enough to heat her up, but not long enough for her nips to get the memo.

"If you're sure," he said, perhaps a bit cautiously. "I didn't see you," he repeated. "Not sure how I missed the shopping cart."

"Um, I think the evidence indicates you absolutely did *not* miss my shopping cart."

He grinned. It was beautiful. "Good point. Let me get someone to clean up this mess. Can you wait here so no one steps in it?"

"Sure thing. I'm due a little community service anyway after the thing with the guy and his nuts in the produce section." Oh God, she was babbling. Stupidly perfect man. No one should be that flawless—it wasn't right.

He scrubbed a hand across the faint stubble on his chin. "There was a thing with a guy and his nuts? In the produce section?"

"Yeah. But there's just a thing in the pickle aisle now and…" She pointed to her shirt. Her shirt pointed back. "So, maybe hurry?"

"Done. Just…don't touch the glass, okay?"

"Got it." More greatness. Not only had she been rel-egated to serve as the wet floor sign, but she was so much of a disaster that Green Eyes could see it from a mile away. Too bad he hadn't seen *her* so readily. And not just because she might have avoided the pickle juice debacle. Being no-ticed by a guy like him was every woman's wet dream. She watched appreciatively as he walked off, all drool-worthy six-foot-something of him. Broad shoulders, narrow waist. V lines for days, she'd bet. A live stream of sweat traversing that man's chest and abdominals would put Netflix out of business.

But that's all she could do—watch appreciatively. She had a life to get back to. Important responsibilities she couldn't let go of. Not to mention she loathed New York City, so falling for one of its inhabitants was just asking for trouble.

Look at her. One minute with Mr. Ridiculously Good-Looking, and she was acting like he'd just proposed marriage. She should know better. Anyone who looked air-brushed in real life had to have a serious flaw somewhere—chronically unemployed, a con artist, or living in his mother's basement. Or gay, which wasn't a flaw, per se—just a disappointment for straight women everywhere.

While she waited for the inevitable "cleanup on aisle four" to hit the PA, she studied the contents of her shopping cart. She needed wine. Lots and lots of wine. And laundry detergent. She had no idea if the machines in the apartment laundry were high efficiency, but the hope seemed a bit am-bitious. The spacious apartment her brother promised her had turned out to be a one-room studio with an excellent view of a rusty fire escape. It had nothing on home, with its rolling mountain views and, most importantly, her parents' memorial garden. Started by her mother as a community green space, the plot, which burst with seasonal blooms and butterflies, had been one of Estelle's favorite spots as a child. When her parents passed away six years ago, her mother's vision lived on through that garden, which bore her name and Estelle's father's. Estelle treasured every moment she spent among the thriving perennials and trees, most of which her mother had placed there herself.

The city made a miserable comparison, no matter how attractive some of its inhabitants.

Thanks to the heat-tinged blood cartwheeling through her veins, she knew Green Eyes was near her orbit before she saw him. She glanced up, barely registering the teenager with the mop and bucket who accompanied the gorgeous stranger.

Forget wine. She needed the hard stuff.

Once she was sure the kid had the scene secured and the green-eyed Boy Scout was preoccupied gathering shards of glass, she made a U-turn in the middle of the aisle and headed off in search of the remaining necessities, only a little disappointed her departure had gone unnoticed but mostly relieved to get out of his line of vision. It was just her luck to meet the god of all sex gods while smelling of pickle juice and sporting a see-through T-shirt.

She found the laundry detergent—high efficiency, just in case—and despite a craving for something a little stronger, she hit the wine aisle pretty hard. She'd need it to keep cool in that sweltering apartment.

She'd need it to forget about that sweltering *man*.

Five minutes later, she was in the checkout line with a cartload of nothing that would make a meal. Stupendous. There was always takeout, she supposed. She paid and the bag boy, who hadn't quite stared at her pickled boobs the *entire* time he'd bagged her groceries, offered to help her to her car.

"No thanks," she said. "I've got…" Oh, hell. She had a problem. A big one.

She didn't have her car. It was on the other side of the country, parked on a concrete driveway in an oasis of lovely single-family homes with large grassy yards, where Spaghetti-Os weren't considered produce.

The bag boy stared expectantly at her.

Behind her, in the line she should by now have vacated, the woman with the toddlers glared, oblivious to the fact that her two little darlings were tearing into bags of Skittles. The candies pinged all over the floor.

"I've got the bags."

The response wasn't hers. She looked up in surprise as Green Eyes swooped in and grabbed everything but the wine. Was he a stupidly handsome serial killer trying to follow her home? She was torn between whacking him with her purse and swooning when he began to walk away from the check stand. "Hey, wait."

He didn't look back, and it was a good thing. Her attention was involuntarily pegged on his ass, and she didn't want to be caught staring. She'd had enough embarrassing moments for one day.

She picked up the wine and jogged five strides to catch up to him just outside the door. "Um, hi there."

He flashed a grin. "Hey."

She started seeing spots, like she'd just stared at the sun. "Those are my groceries." *Please give them to me and go away before I make an idiot of myself.*

"I know. I feel like a jerk for what happened earlier. Let me take them to your car. It's the least I can do."

"Well, my car is a few thousand miles from here." She gestured wistfully toward the west and California. "I don't think the ice cream will make it."

He shifted the bags in his arms, causing his biceps to ripple. Perfectly. "Okay, so that's probably not the least I can do. How are you getting these home?"

"I don't know. Maybe I can leave some on the sidewalk and come back for them." As if. Even *she* knew better than that.

He laughed. It was beautiful. Straight white teeth and a smile that made heavenly choirs sing.

"You can't leave anything on the sidewalk," he said. "It'll be gone in a minute."

"Well, that's just a ringing endorsement for this neighborhood, isn't it?"

He cocked his head. "Let me walk you home. Carry some groceries."

Tempting. *Soo* tempting. His was the only smile she'd seen since her plane touched down, but rather than soothe her rattled, city-hating nerves, it spiked her suspicions. "Wait a minute. You don't even have any groceries. What were you doing in the store?"

"I heard there was a thing with a guy and his nuts in produce."

She blinked. "And that interested you?"

He laughed again. She waited expectantly for one of those beams of light to break through a cloud and spotlight him—he was just that amazing to look at—but there were no clouds. Just a hundred-and-thirteen degrees of sun radiating off a dirty, smelly city sidewalk.

"Scratch that," he said. "I was trying to be charming, and that came out wrong. Truth is, I didn't get your name, so I ditched my grocery list and stalked the exit until I saw you."

"Stalked is not the best word choice here, especially considering you're talking to someone who absolutely hates the city and everything in it."

He tilted his blond head toward her, leading with his ear. "Come again?"

"I hate New York. There, I said it." She braced herself. New Yorkers as a whole didn't seem to get the fact that their city sucked.

He straightened, shooting her a look that clearly conveyed his disbelief. "No one hates New York. That's not possible."

"I do."

"But…great theater. World-class museums. Indie bookstores in every neighborhood. The best pizza this side of the Atlantic. What's not to love?"

"Smog, lack of sunshine, perpetually angry people with a sarcasm problem, and all the bloody traffic." She ticked off all the reasons on the knuckles of the hand holding the wine. "Chewed-up gum covering every conceivable surface. No ocean. And notice I didn't even mention the Yankees yet. Oh, and Donald Trump's hair."

He staggered in an exaggerated fashion, as if she'd hit him. "I should drop your groceries and run, since you just ripped my heart out and stomped on it, but I accept your challenge to prove that our fair city isn't that terrible. Just to show that not all of us are—how did you put it?—angry people with a sarcasm problem, I'll carry these home for you. I assume you came from an apartment?" When she nodded warily, he continued. "Don't worry—I'll wait outside until you make the last trip upstairs. I won't be any different than the dozen other people who see you walk into the building, and you won't have to choose between your ice cream and your wine."

"That's very nice of you, but your charm is wasted. I'm stuck here for two weeks and am literally counting the minutes until my flight home."

"All the more reason to have some guilty pleasures on hand, then, isn't it?" He flashed another stupidly perfect grin. "Lead the way, country girl, and I'll follow."

Chapter Two

Crosby trailed a step behind the grocery store goddess, who kept looking over her shoulder like she thought he'd take off with her bags. Clearly she hadn't exaggerated her dislike of the city and everything in it, which made her temporary stay a good thing. He could get a little too used to looking into those blue eyes, and he didn't time have for her kind of distraction. Not with the weight of his family business on his shoulders. As the oldest of four sons, he needed his focus there. Not on her. But he couldn't help his appreciation, even if she carried herself like she could take him out at any moment with one of those wine bottles.

"My name is Crosby, by the way."

She shot him another look, then slowed a step, allowing him to catch up. "Estelle. And thank you for the help. I can't believe I didn't think about how I was getting all this stuff back to the apartment."

"Maybe it was the thing with the pickles?"

She awarded him with a guarded smile. "We should definitely blame it on the thing with the pickles."

We. One stupid word, but still, now *they* had a thing, and he liked that. He'd like to have much more of a thing with her, but he was already following her home from the grocery store. That was only cute for stray animals, and rarely then. But the woman had stunned him, and not just because he hadn't seen her on the floor under the shopping cart that he also had not seen. It was her eyes. Had to be. They were an exquisite blue, the color insanely deep when offset by the platinum streaks in her stick-straight, glossy blonde hair.

"What are you doing in town?" he asked. He felt like he had to walk a fine line between being friendly and making her think he was one of those guys who made lampshades from human skin. Considering the bizarre track record of their short acquaintance, he wasn't sure he teetered on the preferred side.

"My brother went to some tech writer's conference and didn't want to leave his apartment empty. He sold me on an exciting vacation in the city." She drew to a stop in front of an ancient brick building and looked up, her sapphire eyes decimating him. "Do I *look* excited to be here?"

Well, parts of her did. Two parts, to be exact. His gaze must have drifted the wrong direction because she spun away and headed for the building's front door.

He followed, trying unsuccessfully to suppress a grin.

Inside, the old building actually had a lobby, where a sizable open space held a bank of mailboxes and an elevator. Off to one side, a fire door marked the entrance to the stairs. A single, long-dead potted tree held court, and he noticed her gaze linger on it.

She pressed the button for the elevator then looked

over at him. "If you actually want to wait, I'll be right back."

"I actually want to wait."

"Okay, but if Earl runs you off, don't take my groceries with you."

Before he could tell her that he knew Earl—everyone knew Earl—she frowned at the elevator and stabbed the button again, startling him into silence with her ferocity. "Older gentleman. Told me upon my arrival that he owned the building, but I'm pretty sure it's been days since he's suffered a close call with running water, so I'm not buying it."

"Unlikely story," he agreed. "This building really should have a lock on it."

"It really should have a working elevator." She kicked the closed doors.

"I'm not sure that will help," he said mildly.

"Sure it did. You have no idea how much better I feel. And now I'm taking the stairs."

"I'll be here," he said. "Unless you want help."

"Forget it, Boy Scout. I'm not that convinced of your innocence." She walked up to him, took the bag with the ice cream in it, and flashed another one of those smiles that would put the sun to shame. He caught a faint whiff of pickle juice when she turned, and he didn't even try to hide his grin as she walked away, phenomenal ass swaying like a summer breeze.

Lord knew he could use one of those right about then.

He set the bags on the floor and flexed his fingers while he waited. The woman had odd taste in food. Bread crumbs, jalapeños, potatoes, yogurt, Cheez-Its, microwave popcorn, hot dog buns, laundry detergent, and brown sugar. Plus ice cream and wine. A *lot* of wine.

She also had an incredible body, especially her breasts as

viewed through a wet shirt. Which was precisely what he was thinking about when the door to the stairs swung open and she stepped into the lobby.

"Do I want to know why you're smiling?" she asked.

"Probably not," he admitted.

She blew a few strands of hair out of her face, but they didn't go anywhere. "The stupid air conditioner is about as useful as the elevator. I finally got it to cut on, and I'm not sure it's not blowing heat."

"I can take a look at it for you."

"Do you have a merit badge in coolant or something?"

"You do realize I'm not actually a Boy Scout?"

"Well, I don't see any shining armor. What are my other options?"

"The air conditioner," he said. "I'm—"

"Seriously not getting into my apartment. But nice try." A flirty grin softened her words. She grabbed everything but the laundry detergent. "Be right back."

He watched her go. *Damn*, what a view. He could only imagine the stupid look he must have on his face. He'd have to come up with a way to eradicate it before any of his brothers saw him. He was the only one of the bunch who hadn't brought at least one woman home to their mother's weekly Sunday dinners in ages, but it was as much the family's fault as it was his. As the oldest son, the weight of carrying on the generations-old business fell exclusively in his lap and on his shoulders and everywhere else it could land. The pressure was immense. Eighty years of tradition weighed a fucking *lot*. A gorgeous blue-eyed distraction couldn't have come at a worse time…for him. Or his mother. She'd sent him to the store for ingredients to finish off the desserts for tonight's

Sunday dinner, and so far he was late and empty handed.

Except for laundry detergent.

Which wasn't even his.

He leaned against the brick to wait. The surface was surprisingly cool, which more than made up for the uncomfortable texture. When Estelle popped out of the stairwell doorway, he didn't miss the visual tour she took of his body. She seemed to have relaxed a notch. Her steps were slower. A little less frantic.

A slow smile crept across her lips. She looked pointedly at the detergent parked between his feet but made no move to go down there after it. "Um, thank you?"

"There's a coffee place around the corner," he said. "Can I buy you a cup?"

"Is that what people around here do when they get sweaty? Buy hot drinks?"

He reached to ease a strand of wet hair from her face, and the barely there contact sent all of his blood rushing to his jeans. "The shop is air conditioned. And they sell cold stuff, too."

"Good for them. I told you, I'm not sticking around. And while you seem nice enough, I've seen enough New-York-based television to know meet-cutes in this city never end well."

Rejected based on media portrayal…that was a first. He should be thrilled she denied him. He was forever tied to the city she hated, and he had zero time to get involved with anything other than his job, but her rebuff didn't draw his attention from her eyes, or the way her pupils dilated when he touched her. His fingertip burned with the promise of touching her more, and in more places, and if the way she'd swayed into the contact meant anything, she wasn't entirely opposed to the idea. But that didn't make it a good one.

She'd probably hate that they agreed on that point. But she was also the first one to distract him from his work in a long time, so while it was a good thing she had one foot on the plane, he couldn't put a lid on not wanting to say good-bye.

"So. See you sometime?" Despite his best intentions, it came out in the form of a question requiring a response, instead of the polite brush-off he should have delivered.

"Forgive me, but I'm new here. When a complete stranger stalks a girl in the grocery store—after a minor assault, I might add—steals her groceries, and subsequently follows her back to her apartment building, is it customary to entertain the idea of seeing him again?"

"I *carried* your groceries."

Her eyes glittered with amusement. "And *that* is the only point on which you take issue?"

"I choose my battles."

"Well, I'm afraid you've lost this one, but I do appreciate the help. Do I need to tip you or something?" she asked, effectively dismissing him.

Wow. Obviously it was time to leave Ms. I'm-Country-Y'all alone. "No. I wasn't helping you so I could take your loose change."

"Okay then." She edged backward toward the door to the stairwell. Her eyes skated the length of his body a time or two, but her apparent interest didn't slow her escape. "Have a good day."

The door slammed on her parting words, but he could only grin. She might not want to see him again, but she probably wouldn't have much choice.

He lived in that building, too.

Chapter Three

Sleep eluded Estelle, and as much as she wanted to blame it on the crapped-out air conditioner, she couldn't. Not with electricity crackling off her hand like she was some kind of wizard. Just because Crosby had held that hand to help her off the grocery store floor. Anything more, and she'd have fallen into convulsions. She didn't know what it was about him that got under her skin, but the feeling was as thrilling as it was practically unfamiliar. She hadn't met anyone in ages who had captured her interest like he had.

Pity she was leaving. Faced with two weeks of talking to the walls, she found herself more intrigued with Crosby by the minute.

And more boxed in by the city. The heat was stifling in the small apartment, and no amount of pressing buttons on or even beating the air conditioning unit provided the slightest bit of relief. Eventually, she gave up and opened the window a crack, then jumped back with a yelp when she noticed a miniature, obviously deranged werewolf sitting on the other side of the glass.

Not a tiny werewolf. The world's ugliest cat crouched on her fire escape, staring at her with acid-yellow eyes like he was waiting for her to die so he could come in and calmly eat her face off. The dirty window did nothing to help the feline's sketchy appearance, which could best be summarized as a one-eared, two-fanged explosion of inexplicably fluffy dingy white and black hair. Was that an overbite? Could cats have overbites?

"Off you go! Shoo!" He didn't blink when she whapped the window unit that lay idle next to him. Didn't even flinch. He just sat there, staring, ready to go all *Pet Semetary* on her ass when she least expected it. *Great.*

She pulled down the blinds and tried to go back to bed, but she could have sworn she sensed that cat still sitting there. Waiting. She fell into a half-hearted doze, interrupted by dreams of being followed by many pairs of acid-yellow eyes. In between bouts of sleep she thought about a project she had waiting back home. The client fought her on every detail, right down to the height of the trees…as if Estelle could predict the exact mature height or find a dozen from the nursery that had the same arrangement of branches.

By morning she needed coffee, and lots of it. Naturally, there wasn't a bean to be found in the apartment, since that was one of the things she'd forgotten at the store. While she didn't particularly want to brave the sidewalk, or the Monday morning swarm of New Yorkers crowding it, going without caffeine wasn't an option. And she probably wouldn't have to venture far—coffee shops were everywhere, weren't they?

"Just a quick trip out," she said aloud to absolutely no one. The apartment was small and lonely. Less than twenty-four hours stuck in this god-awful place, and she was about to go crazy. She needed someone to talk to. And grass under her bare feet and views of the sprawling hills. Not brick and concrete and mortar and asphalt and every other cold, unfriendly surface in existence.

She needed a friendly face, but she'd settle for caffeine.

Determined to at least have that, she pulled her hair back into a ponytail and grabbed her purse. She'd shower later, when she had her fix and felt human again.

When she exited the apartment, she was surprised to see someone step off the elevator. Like almost everyone else she'd met in the city, the woman didn't meet her eyes, which was for the best. Estelle was a hot mess, but with the elevator back in service, at least she wouldn't have to take four flights of stairs. Things were looking up. Feeling somewhat buoyed, she stepped through the open doors and hit the button for the lobby. The doors creaked dutifully closed, and with a slight lurch, the car dropped, reminding her of just how very much she *hated* elevators. If she could function without coffee, she'd have realized that before it was too late.

"Just three floors," she muttered. A thirty-foot drop, unless the place had a basement. "You got on a plane, so you can handle an ele—"

A loud metal-on-metal screech wrenched the air. The lights flickered, and the elevator shuddered to a stop. The next second, the car plunged into darkness. A weak emergency light did a poor job of remedying that.

This was it. She was going to die in this miserable city. Without caffeine.

The control panel had a little alarm button on it, but she was afraid to move. And equally afraid to die there. Not convinced the morbid thought was an exaggeration, she bolstered her nerve and edged along the wall just far enough to hit the button with an outstretched fingertip. And…nothing. *Great*. She took another step and jabbed harder. This time she heard a faint click. Was it a silent alarm? Screw that. She dug her phone out of her purse and tapped in a call to 911. After relaying what she could remember of the building address, she resumed her clutch-the-wall-and-hope-for-the-best position and waited. If she survived, she was going to kill her brother. And Crosby, if she ever saw him again. She might have remembered coffee if she hadn't been forced to finish her shopping with a pickle-wet shirt, and if she hadn't been thinking about him all night, she probably wouldn't have been so zombied-out that she actually set foot in this contraption.

She thought about firing off a text to Grady, but didn't because she didn't want to worry him. Still, she was nearly convinced that he *deserved* to worry for putting her in this hell when a muffled, indistinguishable shout echoed into the car. A moment later, the elevator lurched. She grabbed the walls, convinced she was about to plummet to her death, but instead the lift rumbled a couple of feet upward, and the doors jerked open unevenly. Blissful light pierced the darkness as a fireman in turnout gear peered inside. "Everything okay in here?"

"I'm sure it's better out there," Estelle said, accepting the firefighter's proffered hand. There was only a three-inch offset in the floor height, so the assistance wasn't necessary, but she appreciated the chance to gather her wits.

She waved off medical assistance, instead seeking the stairs. She voice-Googled coffee on the way down and was pleased—for once—to learn there was a place less than half a block away. Good thing, because the way her luck ran, catching a cab was not going to happen. On her way in, she'd needed her brother to do it for her, which was ridiculous because the airport had a whole fleet waiting for fares. But she hadn't known what to say and had been terrified of ending up upstate somewhere with a bill that rivaled her mortgage payment, so Grady had done the talking. And bless him, he'd had the decency to look worried.

Estelle had the urge to kiss the sidewalk when she finally made it outside, but between the abundance of used gum stuck everywhere and the overwhelming stench of the city, the impulse passed quickly. A quick glance at her GPS suggested she was headed in the right direction, and within moments, she was inside java-scented heaven. She ordered an iced coffee and a pastry, and just as she reached in her pocket to pay, the hairs on the back of her neck stood. And tingled.

"I've got this," said a deep, familiar voice.

Estelle turned to find herself mere inches from Crosby. His hair was damp, as if he'd just stepped out of the shower, and the lure of his soapy scent was far more seductive than coffee had ever been.

While she stood, dumbstruck, he paid for her breakfast. Dammit. She'd lost the window of refusal. Plus, now that he was there, blaming him for her sleepless night and admitting he'd done that to her seemed a bit counterintuitive to the whole leave-me-alone agenda.

"Thank you," she managed. "But I thought I told you I

wasn't interested."

"You don't have to be, but I do have one question." He said the words as he walked away, which was probably some reverse psychology thing to make her follow. And it worked.

He sat at a table.

She stood facing him. "What's your question?"

"Are you going to sit?"

"Is that your question?"

"No. My question is whether you're going to tell me every time you see me that you're not interested. I heard you the first time, and I don't think men like rejections any more than women do."

Well, that did the trick. Guilt-ridden and grateful for a familiar face, she took the seat across from him and spilled her guts. "I'm sorry, Crosby. It's just… I hate this place," she confessed. "There isn't a living soul to talk to. I got stuck in the elevator on my way down this morning, and there's something scary on the fire escape. And I still have twelve days left."

"Didn't see that coming." His shook his head, an easy smile toying with his lips. "And I'm sorry you're having such a rough go of it."

"I never expected I'd love trading green space for a concrete jungle, but the reality of being here for two weeks staring at the walls is depressing."

"Staring at the walls? You've gone shopping, had an elevator adventure, and I don't know what's going on with the fire escape, but it sounds intriguing." He took a sip of his coffee and grinned. "I told you—you have the city all wrong. There's plenty to do. More than you could ever do in twelve days. And that elevator is notorious. Take the stairs from here on."

"Wait. What do you mean it's notorious? How would you know?"

"We're neighbors. Third floor."

"Oh." She wasn't sure what to make of him not mentioning that the day before.

"And lest you worry, let me assure you I'm no more interested than you are," he said, handily throwing back those shards of rejection. "I was just trying to be nice in the wake of the disaster I caused."

"Well, then," she said. So much for a friendly face. "Thanks again for breakfast. I should go."

She pushed back her chair, only to freeze when his hand landed on her arm. His brow furrowed. "Why are you in escape mode? Didn't I just diffuse this situation?"

"I just thought…"

"That you needed to get back to your empty apartment and stare at the walls?"

Her cheeks heated. "Right."

"And do you think you'll ever not hate the city if you spend the next twelve days doing that?"

"What else am I going to do?"

"You're going to learn to love New York."

She actually laughed out loud. "Don't bet on it."

"Actually, I think we should."

"Not a chance you'd win that one. I thought you New Yorkers were supposed to be more savvy than that."

"Nice attempt at deflection, but it didn't work. I bet by the time you get on that plane, I can make you love no fewer than five things about this place."

"It's not possible."

"It might be a challenge," he admitted. "Especially with my work schedule, but I'm willing to make the sacrifice. In the name of this great city, of course."

"And this isn't a date?" Skeptical wasn't the word for it. She wasn't buying.

"You're a beautiful woman, but I'm married to my job. Additionally, I suck at relationships and you're not staying. We're clearly in agreement that anything more than a friendship is a bad idea."

He looked sincere enough, and she would probably go crazy if she didn't get out of that apartment. How bad could it be?

"Okay," she said. "You're on. Five things, or your city will forever live in miserable infamy, at least with me. And good luck. You're going to need it." She held out her hand, and he shook it.

Crosby was asking for trouble. He couldn't believe how beautiful Estelle was with her casual ponytail and fresh face. She looked like anything but New York, and until he'd laid eyes on a woman his age who didn't insist on painting every inch of her face, he'd had no idea how much he'd appreciate it.

It was a good thing she was leaving. He may still have work on his mind, but he didn't harbor any illusions. No way he'd forget about her just because he was on the clock.

"So why do you work so much when you live in such a fantastic place?" she asked. "Your words, not mine."

"Family business," he said. "If I screw up, it affects us all.

I don't want to be that guy."

"I know the feeling. I'm self-employed, and there's no such thing as taking a break. Not unless you do it with the pressure of a thousand things to do wrecking your good time."

"Exactly." Figured the first woman who'd ever come close to understanding him had to live…somewhere else. "Where are you from, exactly?"

"Weaverville. Middle of nowhere, northern California." She laughed at his surprise. "What? Not everyone from California lives in L.A."

"And not everyone in New York is a jerk."

Her eyes narrowed playfully. "Fine. So far you are not a jerk. But under the circumstances, how are you going to get away from work long enough to redeem the entire city?"

On cue, his phone beeped. He glanced at the display. *Running late* , his brother wrote. *Can you cover me @10?* He welcomed the distraction. Almost wished it had come sooner, because what the hell was he doing with Estelle? "My brother owes me one," he said. Or a hundred…but one would suffice. "I need to get to work." Crosby was supposed to go over the books that morning, but he suspected the chore wouldn't deliver good news.

"You think you can steer me back in the general direction of the building before you abandon me?"

"Careful there, Miss California. Sounds like you might be warming to me."

"You *did* promise to save me from the confines of that apartment."

"I think you're reaching, but I'll take it." He picked up his coffee and swiped the table with a napkin before tossing his trash and opening the door, then settled in step with Estelle for the short walk back to the building. He didn't need to go up to his apartment, but he offered to walk her to hers. "Want me to ride up with you?"

"In that elevator? You must be kidding."

He laughed. "Can I walk you upstairs?"

"No," she said. "You still don't need to know which apartment is mine, but you're getting closer."

He shook his head and laughed. "Fair enough. I'll see you later."

"Twelve days."

"Got it." He watched appreciatively as she let herself inside, not moving from the spot until he couldn't see her anymore. Then he walked to his truck, sitting in its rented parking spot in a private lot a block away. She might have twelve days, but he didn't. His parents and brothers depended on him to keep the business running, which meant he had zero days. What had he gotten himself into?

And why did he have to like it so much?

Chapter Four

When Estelle returned to the apartment, iced coffee in hand, it wasn't yet ten and the air was already scalding hot. She stripped down, trading her tee for a tank top, and stopped short of her plans to open the window. That Hell Cat, or whatever it was, terrified her. If she had to decide between opening the window to that ugly thing and sweating to death, she just might choose the sauna. Other people *paid* for saunas, so how bad could it be?

She pushed back sweaty bangs and, five minutes later, decided she preferred air. Cat-free air.

Warily, she peeked between the blinds and jerked backward at the first shadow, even though it wasn't remotely feline-shaped. A second peek confirmed no cat in sight, so she cracked open the window, disengaging four locks to do it. Maybe the cat would come back, but she needed air, so she took her chances. The other window, she noted, was bolted in place around the air conditioner. The damned thing had proven utterly useless, but she hit the power button anyway, surprised by the whirring sound that immediately emanated from the machine. She'd had to kick it the day before to get it to make noise, so things were definitely looking up.

Until it started spewing smoke.

"Oh, crap." She yanked the cord out of the wall and stood back, expecting…what? An explosion? Flames? Aside from a few dying tendrils of smoke, nothing happened. Keeping one wary eye on the unit, she slid the other window open all the way and crossed to the kitchenette to grab her phone. Grady had left the building super's name and number on the fridge in the event she had any trouble, and this definitely qualified.

She dialed.

The phone rang about ten times before anyone answered, and *anyone* sounded pissed. "What?"

"Um, I'm in 4B and the air conditioner…isn't working," she said in her best I'm-a-friendly-and-low-maintenance-Californian voice.

"We don't have air conditioners."

She stared at the unit. "I'm pretty sure I see one. I mean, there's a little snowflake on it and everything."

"No, lady. What I mean is we don't provide them. If your air conditioner has a problem, it's yours, not mine."

"Um, okay." But the words were pretty much useless, because a *click* interrupted them. Line dead.

Air conditioner dead.

And if she didn't find someone willing to come over and fix it at a moment's notice, she was going to sweat into a puddle, die, and get her face eaten off by Hell Cat.

Great.

She consulted the list of numbers on the fridge, hoping against hope there'd be a HVAC tech on it somewhere. And for once she lucked out. *Fusion Air*. She might owe her anal-retentive-about-everything-but-housekeeping brother an apology. It could soften the blow when he found out how much he owed her for getting the A/C fired up. Repairs weren't cheap. She kept a close eye on the unit as the phone rang. Fortunately, the smoke seemed to have dissipated.

A completely pleasant woman took her call and her info, promising someone would be out by one o'clock. Estelle thanked her profusely, double-pleased when the woman graciously said it was a pleasure to serve her. Okay, score one for Crosby and his miserable city, but he didn't have to know that.

After she hung up, she poked around for a fire extinguisher. She found one under the sink and made a mental note of it just in case the air conditioner spewed a new batch of smoke. Lord, she could use some fresh air — the kind without humidity, smog, or smoke. Or that smell. Garbage trucks back home smelled better than the average New York street.

When she turned from the kitchen, she saw something more terrifying than any of the aforementioned stenches.

Freaking Hell Cat.

In the apartment.

She bit back a scream.

The creature stared placidly, its one remaining ear kicked back in a show of minor irritation. Yellow eyes were nearly lost to a tangle of long gray hair, but the crooked fangs stood out. And scared her shitless.

She glanced around the small kitchen area, her gaze landing on a newspaper. For heaven's sake…who got paper newspapers anymore, Grady? She grabbed it and edged toward the cat, holding the rolled-up pages out like a weapon.

Hell Cat regarded her without interest. Or so she thought. Slowly, she became aware that the low rumble she heard wasn't from the street below but, rather, from her feline house guest. And apparently she'd crossed a line, because the undertone turned into a shrill warning that had her backpedaling against the wall. So much for shooing him out.

When she was a good ten feet away from him, he stopped yowling.

"You're a jerk, you know that?"

The cat blinked.

Estelle tossed the paper on the counter and picked up the remains of her iced coffee. "I'm not feeding you."

The cup in her hand reminded her of Crosby, but it wasn't as if she'd thought of much else. He had to have some issue that would send a sane woman running for the hills—preferably the hills back home in Weaverville. Yeah, he'd confessed to being a work junkie, but that couldn't be the only thing wrong with him? In fact, her problem with every man she'd met back home was a total lack of work ethic, which made Crosby's self-professed flaw yet another point in his favor. The man was unreal.

Still, he stayed stuck in her head while she waited for the repair guy. Despite expecting it, she jumped a mile when a knock sounded at the door. She shook off lingering images of Crosby's incredible body and peered through the peephole, hoping against hope her brother's air conditioner was about to be rescued.

An entire bottle of wine wouldn't be enough to stave off

the shock that greeted her.

Crosby? He wore a freaking Fusion Air hat, which sat slightly, adorably askew, as if he'd wiped his brow and bumped the hat off center. He'd changed his shirt since that morning, though she barely noticed the Fusion logo over all of that sculpted muscle straining the fabric. He looked more like a repair guy porn fantasy than someone who could exist in real life, but his existence was undeniable. Either he worked for the HVAC place—which explained his offer to look at the unit for her the day before—or he'd murdered some poor *actual* Fusion guy and tossed his lifeless body in a Dumpster somewhere.

She took a deep breath and opened the door.

"Hi," he said.

"Really? Just like that?"

He grinned. "Actually, when the work order came in, I recognized the address and remembered you had issues. I didn't want you forced to have some strange guy in your apartment, so I was all over it."

"So your work emergency this morning…?"

"It was legit, albeit not life or death. One of my brothers got held up on a job and needed someone to cover his next appointment. We take our on-time guarantee seriously."

"So you didn't beat up the real HVAC guy just to get to me?"

A perfectly mischievous, deviously kissable smile traced his lips. "Nah. But if it makes you feel any better, I would."

"That absolutely does not make me feel better." *It makes me feel like tearing your clothes off with my teeth.* It would be a kindness, of course, because it was damned hot in there. And suddenly forecast to get a hell of a lot hotter. She could only resist so much, and now fate had put the man in her apartment. She was crumbling, and fast.

"I mean it in the good way. What's the air conditioner doing?"

"Smoking."

"Smoking?"

"Yeah, like actual smoke. I unplugged it. And I have a fire extinguisher."

"It's been an hour since your call. If the unit isn't smoking now, you probably don't have anything to worry about. Now may I come in, or would you prefer to bring the air conditioner to the hallway?"

"I can do that?" As if. The thing was so bolted in, she feared the wall would come down with it, like the aftermath of a failed Jenga move.

"If it makes you more comfortable."

"No way. Come on in. I have the cat."

His gaze followed hers, then widened when it settled on the feline. The creature had not moved since he'd planted his butt on the table. He might have been asleep, but she didn't want to get close enough to look for those yellow eyes in that mess of hair.

"What is that thing?" Crosby asked.

"You mean besides scary? He came in through the fire escape. I assume he belongs to someone, but probably not my brother. Grady's allergic."

"He wouldn't have told you ahead of time if he had a cat?"

"You'd think, but he also told me the fridge was stocked, and it held nothing but ketchup and a single carton of left-over Chinese, which, frankly, I'm afraid to touch."

He shook his head. "Well, I can't say you did much better when you went to the store. Sounds like there weren't any hot dogs waiting for those buns you bought."

"Hey, I was cold from pickle juice. I couldn't think." She didn't bother telling him she didn't even like hot dogs. "You try walking through a refrigerator aisle in a soaked shirt."

His attention dropped to her chest, then eased back up in a way that left her feverish. When his gaze met hers, his eyes were dancing. *Dirty* dancing. "You keep reminding me of you in a wet T-shirt," he said, "and this air conditioner isn't the only thing I'll be sweating over."

"Is that a threat?"

"The very best kind."

Oh, hell yes. Pretty please with jalapeños and whipped cream on top. "Well, in that case, do you want to come in? You're letting all the heat out."

He stepped inside and closed the door, then took the time to engage all three locks. Which kind of thrilled her. "You said the unit was smoking?"

"What?" She'd been watching the play of muscle under his shirt while his arms worked the locks. "Oh, yeah. I unplugged it, but there was definitely smoke."

He went to the broken air conditioner and flipped down the front panel to extract a dusty screen. "This didn't help. Filter needs to be clean for it to work, and this is bordering on a dryer lint quilt. I'm going out onto the fire escape to check out the back of your unit."

She nodded and enjoyed the view as he stepped through the open window.

A moment later he came back in. "Well, the bad news is that it's toast."

"There's good news?"

"I have one you can borrow."

"Oh God. Is this the part where I kiss you?"

He whipped off his hat and tossed it, then closed the distance between them and dipped his head dangerously close to hers. "Only if you want to," he murmured. "Because you do hate the city and are counting the twelve days until your departure."

Oh, God. Backpedaling time. Not just because he had a point she'd do well to remember, but because he was *really* close, and she liked it. Too much. Way too much for a woman determined to spend the next two weeks in the friend zone.

Obviously sensing her hesitation, he backed off, but not far enough for her to breathe. No place in the apartment was probably far enough for that. "I'd invite you to wait in my apartment downstairs, but at the moment the working air conditioning is its only redeeming quality. I've torn the place apart to renovate, and it's currently covered in drop cloths and plaster dust. You're welcome to it, though."

She shook her head. "No, thank you. I'll take my chances up here in the heat."

He laid another one of those devastating grins on her, which left her staring at his lips. "I'll be back in a little while with the air conditioner," he said. "I have a feeling after carrying it up four flights of stairs, I'm going to need to cool off."

"Is that the only reason?"

"God, I hope not." He hesitated, still too close. He seemed to be asking a question…one she didn't want to answer.

Shut. Up. He didn't want her. He was just teasing. She knew it, and she was turned inside out anyway. But who wouldn't be? He was definitely flirting, and he was seriously hot. Any red-blooded woman would respond to that... viscerally.

He gave Hell Cat a wide berth as he collected his stuff, playfully flipped his hat back on his head, and made his exit.

Estelle locked the door behind him, then stared at it dumbly. He was coming back. And they'd be alone. *Alone with a bed*. Rumpled from where she'd flopped on it earlier, it lay there in the studio space, teasing and full of possibilities. If Crosby could move as good as he looked, she was in a world of trouble. The best kind.

She was crazy. *Crazy*. Because they'd both agreed not to go there, and everything about going there remained the worst kind of idea. Still, she burned for his touch. Fortunately, logic tunneled through the haze. The knowledge that he could have already hacked her to bits, had that been his intention, offered little comfort. Being near him put her under some kind of spell, judgment skewed to hell and back. Determined to make at least one decision with a clear head, she made a beeline for her laptop and hit Angie's List. In no time, she found that the existence of Fusion predated widely available conditioned air. They dealt with all things HVAC—heating, ventilation, and air conditioning—and boasted a shiny "A" rating and glowing reviews. No hacked-up customers.

But how many did he flirt with?

She shouldn't have cared, but dammit, she wanted that to be for her. Not because she was some kind of obsessed whacko, but because as a woman, she wanted to know *she* had been the one to do that to him. If he handed out kisses like invoices, she'd be wrecked. And not in the good way.

Reluctantly, she tore herself from visions of his hard body and killer green eyes to Google him. Apparently he'd been working the family business since before high school. No college. No wife, no kids, and no arrest record. The guy was as clean as a whistle. And hot as holy hell. Flirting with him felt a little reckless, and she knew she shouldn't. But they were friends, and she was a grown-ass woman. She could handle this.

She picked up the business card he'd left and tapped his cell number into her phone, followed by a short message.

I'm drenched. Hurry back.

She hit send and tugged at her damp shirt. Who was she kidding? He couldn't want her...she was drowning in her own sweat. What she wouldn't give to be back home. Not that she didn't sweat in Weaverville—temps hit the nineties there, too—but there was something about the expansive green mountains that felt a whole lot like paradise.

She toyed with her phone for a moment, then dialed one of the volunteers who spent almost as much time in Estelle's mother's garden as she did. "Hey, Katie. It's me. How are things there?"

"Rain," she said, forlorn. "The weeds are taking over, and the tomatoes are splitting."

There weren't many veggies in the garden, but they all went to families who had trouble paying for fresh produce—people who counted on them. And split tomatoes wouldn't last long. "I've only been gone two days."

"I know. I'm counting the minutes until you return."

So was she. "I'm so sorry to leave you stuck with this. I'll take care of the weeding when I get home."

"In two weeks there won't be anything but weeds," Katie said with a laugh. "We'll take care of it. Just…have fun."

"Not likely," Estelle muttered. "Thanks for everything you're doing."

"You've got it. Just don't forget to come home."

"No problem," she said. "You're not the only one doing a countdown."

Estelle ended the call in a cloud of guilt. She never should have left California. She had a break between design jobs, but the garden was a twenty-four-hour gig. Grady could have locked his doors, she could have stayed home, and her parents' garden wouldn't be on its way to ruin.

But it was, and it was all her fault.

Chapter Five

Crosby winced as his brother's jaw dropped.

"*You* met a woman?" Sawyer said. "I wasn't sure you knew what one was. You did say a woman, right? An *actual* woman?"

"Is there another kind? Wait, never mind. I don't want to know." Crosby shook his head. Sawyer, the second-born of the four brothers, was the prankster of the bunch. After asking such a dumb question, Crosby would probably wake to find an inflatable sex doll in his truck.

"I'm just saying," Sawyer said. "You don't date."

"I don't have time to date! I'm trying to keep Fusion in the black." Easier said than done, and a losing battle at that. It seemed every old building in the city had been retrofitted with massive systems serviced by national companies.

"No one expects you to do that single-handedly."

"Maybe not, but Mom and Dad are depending on me. Oldest son, family legacy, grandfather kept it afloat during

The Great Depression, all that stuff."

"Yet, you may have noticed all six of us are wearing the same shirt."

Yes, but while his younger brothers were happy to have a job, the family business was more of a stepping stone to them. Crosby, on the other hand, had been close to his grandfather before he'd died of a heart attack. His grandfather founded Fusion Air, built it with his bare hands, and nurtured it into one of the city's most successful small businesses. Crosby had loved working alongside his grandfather to keep it going, even bringing a few twenty-first century ideas to the mix, like an online and mobile appointment calendar and a web-based GPS tracker that allowed customers to see exactly how far away their repair professional was.

But after his grandfather had retired and then passed away, his father had made a few poor decisions, and now the company that had belonged to Crosby and his brothers for over a decade was in danger of going bankrupt. And Crosby wasn't about to let go of the company that was not only his livelihood, but the last piece he had of his grandfather.

Crosby's phone dinged. "Which brings me back to my last job," he said as he checked the notification. "It's a small studio apartment almost identical to mine, maybe five-hundred square feet. What do we have sitting around?"

I'm drenched. Hurry back.

His jaw dropped. The innuendo tore through him like a Taser—a feeling with which he was familiar, thanks to his younger brother, who was staring at him like he'd grown another head.

"You okay in there?"

Crosby looked at Sawyer and, upon realizing his mouth hung open, snapped it shut. "Yeah. Just…yeah. Do we have a unit around here or not?"

"There's an 18,000 BTU laying around," Sawyer said slowly, as if he was still trying to get a read on Crosby. "I think it's the smallest we have."

"That's enough to *refrigerate* a space that small."

Sawyer shrugged, the mischievous light in his eyes a direct contrast to the passive gesture. "What can I tell you, big brother? You'll just have to keep her warm."

Not a bad idea under any circumstances other than theirs. Nevertheless, Crosby was still thinking about it two hours later when he hefted the hundred-pound unit past the "Out of Service" sign on the elevator and up four flights of stairs. He knocked with the toe of his boot.

The door flew open, startling him.

"That was quick," Estelle said.

"Would have been faster if the elevator worked."

"Not necessarily," she said dryly.

"Excuse me, excuse me!" a voice called behind him.

Crosby fought to keep his balance as something pressed against his back, causing him to sway with the air conditioner. He caught a sideways glimpse of an elderly woman bustling around in the hallway as he steadied himself and walked in the general direction of Estelle's kitchen table, where he set down the unit and prayed the table would hold the weight.

He'd forgotten all about the cat.

When he looked away from the appliance, he found himself eye to eye with what was indeed the ugliest animal he'd ever seen. A passing glance before hadn't done the creature justice. It had to be her scary fire escape thing. It had actual fangs hanging out of its mouth, and they were as yellow as its eyes. The realization came in the split second before the cat reached out and smacked his nose with a wide paw that felt like a small, furry catcher's mitt.

He jerked backward, nearly stumbling. Then he realized the impact had been soft. No claws. Which meant he probably still had his face.

"You took my kitty!" The old woman from the hall barged through the door and hit him in the head with an oversized straw bag. Unlike her ugly cat, she and her ugly bag packed some punch.

He blinked, seeing stars, and eased down to the floor. "Um, no I didn't."

"My Mortimer never strays from home," the old woman snapped in a shrill, wobbly voice. Crosby didn't recognize her, which wasn't all that strange considering half the tenants in the building were shut-ins. "He certainly wouldn't be in here if you hadn't taken him," she went on.

Estelle knelt next to Crosby and touched her fingertips to the side of his head. "He came in through the fire escape," she said of the cat. Looking toward the woman, she added, "Which is how you're about to leave if you hit *my* guest in *my* apartment again."

The batty old lady faltered for a moment. He couldn't blame her. Estelle's words belied her calm tone, although he barely noticed. She was way too close for him to think about anything other than her body. Suddenly he wasn't sure if the stars he saw were from carrying the unit up four flights of stairs, getting knocked upside the head with a brick of a purse, or the smokin' hot woman crouched next to him.

"Come, Mortimer." The old woman's wrinkled face unwound just a bit as she called to her feline, who placidly hopped from the table, where he had sat the entire time, and nudged Crosby. Unsure of the proper etiquette in such a situation, he tentatively reached out to pet the cat, which in turn nudged hard against his thigh.

Then bit him on the ass.

"OW!" For a moment, he thought he imagined the sharp pain, but after it refused to subside, he knew it was real, and the cat had really, truly bit him on the ass. And smirked at him as he walked off toward his owner.

"Does your cat have all his shots?" he called after her.

"Of course he does. Are you saying I don't take care of my Mortimer? He's like a child to me."

"Your child needs to see a dentist," Estelle said.

The cat jumped into the woman's arms, and she turned with a classic "hmph" and walked out of the apartment. Estelle shut and locked the door.

She regarded him with a hint of bemusement. Either that, or he made too much out of the play at the corner of her lips. "That was hilarious."

"Good for you," he said. "Amusing neighbors. Score one point for me and the city."

Her brow raised. "I'm not sure you get credit for her. Why did you ask about shots?"

"Because the cat bit me."

Estelle rushed over and knelt by him. Her concern totally made the puncture worth it. "Where? When?"

"On the ass," he said, deadpan.

She froze. "Are you serious?"

"I am." She was so close. *And drenched*. He'd yet to

shake her words…or his constant analysis of them. He didn't want to be a jerk and assume they were any kind of invitation, but after a near-kiss that had shredded his ability to think platonically, he couldn't seem to take them any other way. He'd already seen too much. Frankly, he'd let a California grizzly bear have a go at him if it meant she'd touch him again, but he suspected that was poor judgement on his part.

Her expression bordered on studious, none of the heat which he felt apparent in her eyes. "That might need treatment. Let me see."

He nearly choked on her demand. "Let you see my ass?"

She pursed her lips. "Let me see where the cat bit you."

"Which is my ass."

Humor lit her eyes and quirked the corners of her mouth. He was sure this time. "Okay, let me see your ass."

He stood and pulled her to her feet. She landed briefly against him. He steadied her and prayed she couldn't hear his heart hammering in his chest. Forcing calm to his voice, he said, "I'm intrigued by the invitation, but let me get this unit working before we both die of heat exhaustion. It's got to be over ninety in here." *Because you're drenched.*

On cue, she lifted her shirt and fanned her stomach. He had to stop himself from dropping to his knees and pressing his lips to the bared flesh. The heat had to be getting to him. He was normally a fairly sane person. He didn't stand in a thousand-degree apartment and give serious consideration to licking his customers, but Estelle was no ordinary customer.

He tore his attention away from her belly and turned his focus to the broken down A/C unit. He used his adjustable wrench to loosen the bolts holding the old appliance and wrestled it into the apartment, then set the new one in place and had her steady it from the inside while he went out and adjusted the support so it would sit at the proper angle. He was dripping sweat by the time he crawled back inside, but when he plugged in the unit and hit the button, the machine immediately kicked on.

"My hero," Estelle said. "Seriously."

"Until your brother sees his electric bill. Otherwise, it's the least I can do after the pickle thing." He tightened the rest of the bolts and tossed his wrench on the table. He'd left the tool bag in the truck since simultaneously carrying that and the behemoth air conditioner wasn't even worth attempting, and the wrench had fit easily enough in his pocket. And now if he forgot it, he had a great reason to return.

Cool air already infiltrated the apartment, but not quickly enough. He took off his wet Fusion shirt and wiped his face with it, for all the good it did, before laying it over the back of a chair.

Estelle handed him a glass of ice water she'd grabbed from the kitchen and stared at his bare chest. "A little ridiculous, don't you think?"

"What?"

"Your stomach. Overkill, isn't it? Way to make the rest of us feel inferior."

He blinked. Her words registered. And ever so slowly, he returned the favor. With just a fingertip, he eased the hem of her shirt up an inch, then two. "Inferior, my ass. *This* is sexy," he said. "Curves. Soft planes. That's what men go crazy over. A woman might want everything hard as a rock, but a man wants to sink into something soft."

Thick tension filled the silence that followed. She took

a half step back, and he had to force himself not to follow.

She swallowed. "The pickle thing is completely forgiven," she said, her voice a little shaky. "Remember? You bought my breakfast."

Her gaze drifted south of his eyes, and he returned the favor. She wore a thin, hot pink tank top, the platinum streaks in her ponytail wildly bright against her shirt.

She was also holding an ice cube to the base her throat. She probably hadn't meant it as an outright seduction, but the water droplets that escaped and trickled toward her cleavage made it absolutely impossible to be anything less. He was hot in ways that had nothing to do with the temperature. So much so that it took him a minute to realize the blast of skin-prickling heat that assaulted him wasn't the lure of sex, but the window he'd left open. He turned to close it and froze.

The damned cat was back, demurely perched just inside the sash.

"Straight out of a horror flick," he said.

"Window stays open, I think."

He took a long drink of water that was so cold he felt it all the way down. "Agreed," he said when he'd drained the glass. "The window unit can handle it."

"Good," she said, grinning. "Because it's about to get hot in here. Now take off your pants."

Chapter Six

Knowing Crosby's eyes were glued to her every move, Estelle let go of what was left of the ice cube. It dropped immediately to the valley between her breasts, offering the smallest of thrills before the cool sensation dissipated into heat.

"Take off my pants?" He looked a little shocked. Hard to believe these sophisticated city girls weren't more forward, but then again, she wouldn't have been either if he hadn't been bitten in her honor. Or at least in the name of conditioned air.

"Yeah. Cat bite to the ass, remember?"

"The bite is fine."

"You don't want to take off your pants?"

He simply grinned, then crossed the small apartment and swiped an ice cube from the freezer, then came back and touched it to the hollow of her collar bone. "Estelle, if I take off my pants, I can guarantee my ass will be the last thing either of us are worried about."

She shivered, more from the promise than the ice. The look in his eyes wasn't one she'd seen before. On any man. Ever.

He watched her intently as he moved the ice from her neck to the hollow behind her ear to her nape. The cool water dribbled down her back, and she bit back a gasp. The ice was cold and the air conditioner rapidly cooled the room, but neither had any chance against the heat coursing through her body. She'd once stepped barefoot on an electric fence in morning dew, and she was certain it hadn't affected her more than this man.

"Do you have to go back to work?"

A slight frown briefly marred his face but quickly vanished. "No."

"No?"

He shook his head nearly imperceptibly, a whisper of a smile shaping his mouth. "No."

"Want to order a pizza?" she asked. She tried desperately not to stare at his bare chest, but it wasn't working. "It's on me. For the use of the air conditioner."

"And the bite on my ass."

And with any luck, we'll need our strength. "Yeah, that, too."

"I'm guessing you like jalapeños on your pizza?"

"And spinach."

"I'll see your spinach and raise you green olives."

Her nose wrinkled. "Green olives?"

He twisted his face in an expression she suspected mirrored her own and returned the disdain. "Jalapeños?"

"Halvsies?"

"On a white pizza?"

She grinned. "Is there any other kind? Although I have to say I'm shocked. You said you had three brothers. I figured you'd order your pizza with meat topped with meat. You're not a vegetarian are you?"

"Nope. Turns out my brothers all think pizza without meat and red sauce is almost as horrifying as adding all that green stuff, and that if I wanted a salad, I should order a salad. But I stuck with my crazy concoction—crafted entirely due to their accusation of eating *all that green stuff*, which is a quote—and never have to share."

"Until now."

His fingertips curled at her nape, then followed the path the ice until his thumb grazed her jaw. The ice had melted, but his touch had remained. "There are certain circumstances that absolutely require a willingness to share."

She swallowed. Hard. Mentally shoving him back to the friend zone, she asked, "You sure don't want some meat on meat?"

He laughed, breaking some of the spell. Which was excellent, but she was about to throw herself on the bed and pray he'd take the hint. "No way," he said. "And since you hate the city and all its concrete so much, how about we pick up that pizza on the way to some green space? I meant what I said about showing you the other side."

"The very fact that you have to help me find green space supports my hatred."

"Fair enough, but if you miss all that green space as much as you claim, you'd jump at the chance to visit a park."

Damn. He had her there. "You're going to have to put on a shirt."

"I'll grab a dry one from my apartment."

"Deal. I'll order the pizza." She pulled up the app on her phone.

Upon seeing the chain's logo on the screen, he shook his head. "No way. You can have that anywhere. How about something from the city?"

"That's a selling point?"

"You can't say you hate it until you try it."

"Fine." She handed him her phone, though he probably had his close, and tried not to let her eyes linger. She was kidding herself if she thought the shirt would erase from her mind the very distracting vision of his upper body. Even the image from the grocery store lingered, and that was before she knew what lay underneath that cotton tee.

He handed back her phone. "It'll be ready when we get there."

She blinked. She'd missed the whole phone call—a fact *he* probably hadn't missed. She needed to get a grip. Staring all moon-eyed at a hot guy was something teenagers did. She grabbed her keys and decided to forgo her purse, instead slipping her ID and a credit card in the front pocket of her shorts. Carrying a bag around seemed a little too obvious. A little too *rob me because I have all the things in here.*

They stopped at his apartment, which was every bit the mess he claimed. Sheets covered most of the space, with only sparse lumps indicating some kind of furnishing underneath. "Where do you sleep?" she asked.

He pointed to one corner. "Air mattress for now. I have new furniture coming as soon as I paint and put in the new floors."

"Nice," she said.

"It will be." He dug under a tarp and came up with a dry shirt. Her attempt not to ogle him failed.

Just. Friends.

"Where are we headed?" she asked as they exited the apartment.

"Prospect Park, Brooklyn."

She bit back one of those *oh hell no* laughs, a cry for help that she didn't choke out. "*Brooklyn*? I bet the pizza is greener than that place."

He just smiled.

Whatever that meant.

Crosby felt a little untethered as he walked into Prospect Park in the middle of a Monday afternoon. His brothers had promised they could cover for him after he'd texted them, but Fusion was Crosby's responsibility. It didn't matter how often they told him the burden was a shared one—he didn't want to let them down. He didn't want to disappoint his grandfather or fail his memory. That was why he threw himself into his work—that, and he didn't want his brothers to burn out and hate the family business.

But what about you?

He'd never felt burnout before, but he'd never had anything to draw him away from work. No woman had ever caught his eye the way Estelle did. And he did have to concede a point for her. Despite his concern over stepping away from work, his mood changed the minute he entered the park. He loved the city, but even he felt the oasis offered by the green space.

"This place is huge."

"Over five-hundred acres. There's a zoo, wooded trails, an Audubon society, horseback riding, playgrounds…and from the thick of the trees, there's no concrete to be found."

"You really know the way to a girl's heart."

"Is it that simple?"

"Nah. There's also the pizza. Do you spend much time here?"

He shook his head. "I'm usually working." As in, always. The mom and pop market was biting it, big time. Crosby began working weekends for the regular rate and picked up a few new customers, but a single-family home here and there didn't make up for the loss of all the buildings that had shifted to central systems. He'd been on a seven-day schedule for months, only taking off Sunday afternoons for his mother's family dinner.

"You should work less."

"No rest for the wicked. Or people who run family companies." Despite the serious declaration, a smile threatened as he led Estelle to a bench. "I have to warn you, you'll never again enjoy one of those chain store pizzas after this."

"Big talk. And also unfair, because I'm starving."

He flipped open the box and held it while she grabbed a piece, then waited while she took her first bite.

"Oh. My. God." Her eyes rolled back in her head. "This is amazing. You win."

"Worth a visit to the city?" He grabbed a slice, careful to avoid the half with hot peppers.

"Yes. But if you ever repeat that, I'll torture you with jalapeños."

"Fair enough. And for the record, that's two things on

your list of things to love about the city."

"The old woman doesn't count," she said again.

"We'll see. So what do you do out there in the middle of nowhere, California?" He'd wondered, since she said she worked for herself, but he hadn't wanted to scare her off by asking too many questions.

"I'm a landscape design architect. It's a lifelong passion. Apparently I was born hating cities and concrete."

He wanted to disagree. Really wanted to tell her the city wasn't such a bad place, but it was hard to argue with someone who made a career out of designing green spaces—spaces a little larger, he assumed, than the holes created in the sidewalks to hold a lone tree and maybe a couple of sad plants. Granted, there were parks, but all were well established some decades ago. A little further from the city's core, genteel old houses lined postage stamp-sized lawns, but not much with which a landscape architect could make a living. Damned if she was right…there wasn't much in the city for her. And that made him ache, because as much as she had his head spinning, he remained astutely aware of the fact that he wanted to get to know her better but probably wouldn't get the chance.

"Do you come from a long line of landscape professionals?" he asked.

"Not a long line, no. And heaven knows the gene pool wasn't strong because my brother can't keep a cactus from keeling over. But my mom was a landscape architect, and my dad ran a tree service. That was how they met, and they merged their work and formed a company."

"Do you work for them now?"

"No. Grady and I were late-in-life babies. They retired

and sold the business when I was in high school and died a couple years later in a car accident."

"I'm sorry. That must have been so hard for you."

"It was. It is. But my mom designed and funded a bunch of green space for the city—and by *city*, I mean a municipality that's a lot more grass than asphalt—and after they died I took over the largest of the areas and made it a memorial garden. I love it there. Most of what's growing she planted herself. Having that connection through living things helps a lot."

"And I guess when you're in a place like this, you miss that connection more than ever."

She grinned. "Maybe not in a place like *this*. But out there"—she tipped her head, indicating the world beyond the park's borders—"definitely."

They finished the pizza, Crosby only half-dying when a stray pepper found its way onto one of his slices. His surviving half had to admit the peppers were good on the pizza.

He disposed of the box. "Up for a walk?"

"You're not going to toss me in a thicket or something are you?"

"If I did, you'd probably be thrilled."

She laughed and headed off with him in the direction of the forested area. "I'm geeking out over the trees. It's almost embarrassing."

"Don't be. My brother's ex-girlfriend liked to geek out over seven-hundred-dollar shoes and twenty-five-hundred-dollar purses. I think trees are a fantastic improvement."

"I guess that's what made her an ex?"

"Maybe. Liam's young, though. Twenty-six now, and probably not looking to be tied down to a woman who cares more about her closet than she does him."

She slowed to trace her fingertips over a tree trunk. "Ouch. What about the rest of your brothers?"

"Sawyer is next in line after me. He'll never settle down for more than a night. If he's still there the next morning, it's practically a commitment on his part. Ethan was born between Sawyer and Liam. He's the serious type. He married his high school sweetheart only to lose her a couple years later to lymphoma."

"That's horrible."

"It was. It's been three years, and he hasn't been on a date since."

"Has he also thrown himself into his work?"

He frowned. "Sometimes I think he just goes through the motions. He's still in a bit of a cloud."

"So what's your story?"

"I don't have one. Nothing exciting or tragic, at least. I dated in high school and more in the years thereafter, but nothing serious. The more involved I got with learning the business, the less time I had for other things."

"If this is you being antisocial, I can't wait to find out what happens next."

He sidestepped a kid on a bike, grateful to be spared a reply when he found her staring at a tree. They all looked the same to him, but she seemed awed. "Nice tree?"

"Hawthorn." She turned and playfully bumped shoulders with him. "Since we've agreed to just be friends, I'm dying of curiosity. I find it hard to believe you're single."

"I think the mystery here is why *you* are," he countered.

"That's a mortifying subject, you know."

"What's that?"

"Asking a girl why she can't get a boyfriend."

"Estelle, there's no doubt in my mind you could *get* one. My question is why you haven't wanted one."

She rolled her eyes and gave an exaggerated moan. "See, this is why you're so improbably single. You always know what to say, and you seem to mean it. Some girl should snatch you up."

He touched her hand and her fingers immediately laced through his. "Some girl did. At least, for a couple of weeks."

"Ah, so that's it? So all the poor, love struck ladies who can't get over that perfect face of yours were just temporary?"

He actually blushed—and then expertly deflected. "Believe it or not, I wish our friendship didn't have to end so soon."

"Give it time. I guarantee you'll be glad to be rid of me. You have puncture wounds on your butt, and we're only a day in. I don't think you could handle me for an extended period of time."

"I bet you're right, but not for the reasons you think. Now, why haven't you found someone worthy of your time?"

"I'm twenty-eight years old, and I own my own business. Most of the men I meet can barely hold down jobs, or barely want to. Even the ones who spend all day in a suit and tie want to party the second they leave the office. Or surf or work on their tans. It is California, after all. It's like perpetual high school out there, and I want more. I want a man with drive."

"What if he's so wedded to his job that he wouldn't have time for you?" It took him a pathetic moment to realize he could be talking about himself. But he wasn't. Because they were just friends.

"Crosby, look around." She swept her arm across the park vista before them. "You're walking along a tree-shrouded trail in the middle of a Monday afternoon. The right guy makes time."

Her words actually stopped him in his tracks.

She turned to him and grinned. "I'm not saying *you're* the right guy. In fact, you're clearly *not* him, all things considered, which only serves to further my point that, under certain circumstances, you can be peeled away from your job. Just imagine what you'd do for the right woman."

He forced his feet to move. "I suppose you're right."

"Of course I am."

"But not about everything. You have to admit this place isn't as bad as you expected."

"You have one and a half points out of five. Don't count your chickens, buddy."

He choked on a laugh. "We don't count chickens here. That aside, why do you hate the city so much? I doubt the Yankees or Trump's comb-over are really responsible for ruining your stay."

"The crowds. The concrete. The utter lack of breathing room. And for that matter, the air doesn't feel good to breathe. You know those coffee commercials where the person takes a deep breath over that steaming cup and they smile?"

He nodded.

"That's me out of the city."

"And you in the city? Oh, wait, I know this one. *Drenched*, right?"

She froze, staring at him. "You did not just say that."

"No, you did."

Her face turned a shade redder. "That's not what I meant."

"And here I was wondering if you were rethinking our arrangement." He tugged at his damp shirt. It had to be a hundred in the shade. "But misunderstandings aside, you're definitely hot."

"So are you." Her sweet little grin was anything but innocent. He already ached for her, and it was more than physical. He liked her, which felt like a playground confession if ever one existed. So maybe it was better that they'd agreed to keep things platonic, so he could have a little bit of Estelle in his life even after she left New York, instead of ruining things with sex.

But right now, casual sex really didn't seem like such a terrible idea…

Her eyes flew wide at something over his shoulder. "Is that a carousel?"

He didn't have to follow her gaze—he knew where it went. "Yes it is. It's been there over a hundred years." And he'd die if he had to get on that thing, but the wonderment in her eyes suggested she had other plans.

"Can we ride?"

"Of course." Great. He'd never, ever live this down. Maybe his brothers would never find out. "Classic New York experience," he said to Estelle. "I wouldn't dream of depriving you."

His words were wasted. She was already tugging him to the ride, and he wouldn't miss her excitement—or his chance to score another point—for anything. After a brief wait in line, he ponied up the fare and watched, absolutely tortured, while she climbed up and straddled one lucky jackass. He climbed up on the horse next to hers, ridiculous as he felt, and when the carousel started, he was relieved to find his ride was stationary. But the relief was short lived, because having her rise and fall so close to him left him nearly incapable of getting off his horse when it was over. He managed, then tried not to notice how natural it felt to take her hand as they walked away. The image of her laughing and carefree would haunt him for a while. Especially because, for a moment, he'd felt that way, too.

"You finding the city a bit more tolerable now? The antique carousel was so spectacular that we've found thing number three that New York does better than California?" he asked as they meandered through seemingly endless groups of people.

"Nope." She laughed at the shock that must have splayed across his face. "I'm tolerating the park. Not the city. You, on the other hand, I kind of like. What the heck is that?"

He followed her gaze to the enormous concrete ellipse that stretched ahead of them. "Your worst nightmare."

"Seriously?"

"It's a spray park or a water playground or whatever they're called." And popular, too, judging by the swarm of attendees. The large oval was surrounded on all sides by streams of water that arched inward like a school fountain. As they drew closer, the place seemed to expand. He'd never paid much attention to it, so the size caught him off guard. He could only imagine what she thought of the thing.

She looked from the crowd of screaming wet people to him. Mischief sparked in her eyes. "I dare you," she said.

"I'm sorry?"

She cocked her head. "You said you didn't have much fun. So let's have some."

"I'm pretty sure I'm too old for a playground."

"The fact that you think that absolutely convinces me you need to come play with me."

Jesus. All the play he had in mind absolutely did not belong in a public place, let alone one largely populated by kids. But she'd already grabbed his hand and was pulling him toward the spray. "Hang on," he said.

"No wimping out."

"Not wimping. Just saving my cell phone. And maybe my shoes."

She rolled her eyes but joined him in leaving her shoes and cell phone out of harm's way. Then she dragged him in, directly into the falling water. The stream, while not cold, was chillier than he expected. He was instantly not hot… until he took a good look at the woman who had yet to let go of his hand. Nipples on full display. God, they were sensitive. He immediately wondered how she'd react to his mouth on them, then wanted to kick himself. He was not the kind of guy who lived with his brain in the gutter. That was his brother, Sawyer, from whom Crosby couldn't differ more… at least in the dating department. Crosby didn't duck out on work. He didn't kiss his clients, and he didn't stare at nipples. And he didn't know what had changed.

She poked him lightly in the chest. "You know, for a guy surrounded by a bunch of people who appear to be having the time of their lives, you're not looking too happy."

"I'm thinking."

Blue eyes flashed behind silken strands of damp hair. Her shirt, plastered to her skin even before the water happened, clung to every curve. And he wanted her. "About what?" she asked.

"This." He reached with his free hand to cup the back of her head, pulling her mouth to his. Standing in the spray while lightning struck—probably not the best idea, but he devoured her anyway. Water hit the back of his neck and splattered, creating a cloud of raindrops around them. A good thing, considering what he intended as a playful kiss had quickly morphed into an explosion of need best experienced without witnesses. He regretfully broke free, finding her eyes dark with the same desire that had overtaken him.

"Want to go check out the air conditioning?" she whispered.

"I thought you'd never ask."

Chapter Seven

They raced up the apartments stairs. All four flights. *Stupid elevator*. Estelle wrestled her keys out of her wet pocket and unlocked the apartment. When she threw open the door, cold air blasted so hard she took a step back.

"Wow. That's one effective air conditioner."

"Completely my fault. I forgot to mention it's rated for a bigger space." He went over and turned it down. The compressor kicked off, but she felt like a Popsicle in her wet clothes. Her teeth chattered and made it official, leaving her to wonder if Crosby liked Popsicles. And if he ate them with long, slow licks. Or sucked on them. So many possibilities. She shivered. "Maybe open the window for a while?"

"You've got it." He unlocked and raised the window, and blessedly hot air blasted through. "This won't take long."

"Just what a girl wants to hear."

"I stand corrected," he said. "This could take all night." Then he leaned in and planted a toe-curling kiss on her lips.

Chaste enough that absolutely nothing should have curled, but it left her in knots anyway. All of her previous stranger-danger awareness had settled into something deeply sexual. He was a god of a man, and she'd given him the perfect out when she'd asked if he needed to go back to work. And he hadn't taken it. Instead, he'd taken her to the park. He'd wanted her to see his world, and that touched her.

Chills snaked down her spine.

"Still cold?"

"Chilly."

"That's because you're…wet."

"I'm definitely wet."

He was close. So close. His incredible eyes were on her. They were truly an unreal shade of green. She briefly wondered if he'd let her take a picture, but when she imagined that particular shot, it wasn't just him, but also her. Laying against rumpled white sheets, their heads touching and bodies entwined.

Oh, shut up. You can't see all of that in a selfie.

The intrusion of logic didn't stop her from glancing toward the bed, unable to unsee the godawful Star Wars sheets she knew lay under the comforter. Grady was the ultimate geek. He'd promised he'd wash the bedding—and best she could tell by the lingering scent of laundry detergent, he had—but not that the linens were suitable for a grown-ass man.

She never dreamed she'd have one in her brother's apartment, or she'd have replaced the sheets herself—not that it mattered. Anything that happened with Crosby had a definite expiration date. It didn't matter how thoroughly he rocked her. Her life was on the opposite coast. She was a landscape architect, for heaven's sake. She had her mother's garden, and Estelle hadn't earned her master's degree to live in this urban anti-oasis.

"Where'd you go?"

She blinked her way back to Crosby and was immediately lost to the green depths of his eyes. "Right here," she whispered.

He pushed damp tendrils of hair away from her face. "Can I kiss you?"

"You have to ask?" She struggled to stay upright when all she wanted was to fall into him. Her fingertips rested on his stomach, and she worried he'd think she was pushing him away, so she lightly gripped his shirt.

His eyes, still laser bright, had softened, leveling their own kind of seduction on her. He traced the side of her face, then her neck. "Yes, I do."

Oh, *swoon*. "You just kissed me, and you didn't ask first."

"That was different. That's not how I intend to kiss you. I planned something different this time."

He planned? She released his shirt and rested her fingertips on his chest, marveling at how hard he was. But she didn't marvel long before he spoke.

"You didn't answer my question."

Whisper soft, husky, and gentle, his voice melted her. "Kiss me, Crosby."

The words were barely out of her mouth before he had his hands around her waist. He lifted her without effort, then playfully tossed her on the bed, coming down after her. Before she could catch her breath, he was on top of her, all hard under his wet clothes but offering only gentle touches of his rough hands. His well-worn jeans were deliciously coarse against her skin as he moved between her thighs, but it was his mouth that truly did her in. His lips devoured her so softly that a strangled cry caught in her throat. She wound her fingers in his hair, trying to pull him closer, deeper, but she was no match for all that long, lean muscle. He held himself easily, keeping that same slow, explorative pace that had her throwing one leg over his in a futile effort to drag him closer, to feel the sweet relief of any kind of pressure *down there*. He finally relented and the ridge of his erection between her legs nearly did her in.

"Oh. My. God." She fed him the words on a moan.

His lips stretched into a smile against hers. "Is that good?"

She responded by pulling him in for another kiss. This time he wasn't quite so sweet about it. This time he demanded it, which had her imagining all kids of other demands. Naked ones. Ones that would leave them both sweaty despite the air conditioner that, even with the open window, still had the temperature hovering at refrigeration. But she could totally do freezing as long as she didn't have to do it alone.

His kisses moved to her neck, and she turned her head to the side. His fingertips had just found her breasts when she saw it.

The damned Hell Cat was on the bed next to them, all of six inches from her face.

"Jesus." She jerked away, managing to hit her chin on Crosby's forehead.

"What the—"

"The cat," she muttered. "I'm sorry."

He swore a soft oath, at the same time managing to shift them together across the queen-sized bed to eradicate her view of the creature. "Where were we?"

"I think we were being stalked by that demon spawn."

"I think I was about to kiss you again." He angled his mouth over hers.

She wasted no time in granting him entry. She held on as he settled his hands around her waist, giving her brief, thrilling thoughts of being held as he drove into her. One by one, the imaginary scenarios in her head gave way to reality. No longer did she have to imagine the weight of him between her thighs or the thrilling contrast of soft sheets and his hard body. Clothing still covered the important parts, but already the sex was incredible. In her mind, she had gone there. *So* gone there.

He broke the kiss. "Estelle?"

"Got it in one," she said, breathless and not really caring what he called her.

"Funny. Look on my back."

"Um, okay?" She did a slight sit up, pushing him slightly upward in the process, and found herself staring over his shoulder into the yellow eyes of evil.

She fell back against the mattress, more than a little terrified but lacking options. "What is it with you and that cat?"

Crosby shook his head and laughed. That was when she noticed he was holding a plank position over her with what looked like ease. She couldn't do a plank for ten seconds without shaking and sweating like she'd run a marathon, and he looked…relaxed. "Could you, I don't know, move him?" he asked.

"Are you kidding me? He bit you on the ass."

"Which is pretty much my point right now."

"Fine." She forced a mock growl and eased out from under him while he kept his iron-man pose. The cat gave her minimal regard as she climbed off the bed and, circling wide, came up from behind. She couldn't help but notice Crosby's phenomenal ass. And his back. It was a solid plane of muscles, and the furry addition was kind of cute in the *hot guy holds a puppy* kind of way. Only the cat wasn't a little ball of squirmy puppy. It was a freaking sentry of hell, and now she had to touch it.

She glanced at the window. Still open. Before she could talk herself out of it, she grabbed the feline from behind by his kitty armpits and, holding him at arm's length as a growl rumbled from the cat to shake her bones, walked him to the window and gently dropped him onto the fire escape. She quickly shut the window. The cat turned around, sat down in front of the glass, and promptly doubled the intensity of his *evil personified* glare. She locked the sash. Probably should have done that sooner anyway. The locks that studded every possible exit probably weren't there for the aesthetics.

She turned to find Crosby standing behind her and grinned. "Where were we?"

Chapter Eight

Crosby was torn. He wanted nothing more than to touch Estelle. To relish every inch of her body. But she intrigued him in other ways. She was genuine. Free-spirited. She might feel trapped by the small apartment and the concrete walls that marred the view in every direction, but she maintained her sense of humor in spades. He couldn't get through a single day without worrying about the future of his company and she—

Wait.

He *had* gotten through a single day.

This one.

With her.

Which probably meant he'd doomed his grandfather's business to oblivion.

"You're doing it again," she said.

"What?"

"Going all pensive on me."

He shrugged out of his wet shirt and gave serious consideration to helping her out of hers. "What can I say? I'm a thinker."

"Are you thinking about showing me your ass? Because I really should look at that bite."

"Your entire afternoon has revolved around my ass."

"Not yet, but if you want to make your move, we might be able to arrange that."

"Are you sure? Really sure? Because the cat's locked out, my cell phone is off, and that air conditioner isn't likely to catch on fire. We're about out of interruptions."

"I'm really sure."

His mouth was on hers before she finished the sentence. She squealed at his mini-attack, then looped her arms around his neck as he dove in, tasting heaven. He eased her to the sofa, but it was too short, so it thwarted his attempt to get horizontal. He dropped one leg over the edge and used it for leverage, deepening the kiss. The little sounds she made suggested she liked it…at least until his foot hit the coffee table and overturned it, dumping a half full cup of water on the floor.

"Unbelievable," he muttered. It was just one thing after another with them.

He stared at her, faced flushed, lips swollen from his kisses, and could do nothing but shake his head and laugh. After a quick glance toward the mess, he pushed the bulk of it away, then twisted and pulled her down to the floor on top of him. Surprise lit her eyes. Then she ever so fucking slowly leaned down and *licked his nipple*. His dick snapped to attention, and he was half surprised it didn't fling her across the room, catapult style. Thank God he still wore his jeans.

He ached. *Ached.* And that tight little ass of hers strad-dled him, his shell-shocked man of steel lodged between her thighs. By the time her tongue made a tawdry tour of his other nipple, he managed to sit, trapping her with his hands at her lower back. With her straddling him, her breasts were at mouth level. He wasted zero time latching onto one, but the mouthful of fabric wasn't enough. Apparently she felt the same way, because in one lightning-quick move, she jerk-ed off her tank top and left him staring at her bra. No visible hooking mechanism. *Great.* Fortunately she didn't wait for him to do the honors. She reached back and had the gar-ment off with impressive speed.

He didn't waste time on a compliment. Instead, he sucked one tight nipple into his mouth. When she arched against him, jutting that breast further into his face, he al-most came on the spot. Her fingers had a death grip on his hair, and she was moaning and riding him like he was a fuck-ing Clydesdale. He forced himself not to think beyond her breasts. To absolutely *not* think about plunging between her thighs.

He failed on that last point in a very big way.

He switched to the other breast, sucking and tonguing the peak until her every breath formed his name. He felt like he was going to break something in his jeans. Penile fracture was an actual thing, and…screw that. He managed to scram-ble to his feet without losing his hold on her delectable body. He carried her, walking in the general direction of the bed. When his knees made contact he tossed her playfully, land-ing on top of her in time to swallow the squeal that erupted when she bounced on the mattress. He reached and man-aged to unbutton her shorts in one move. He was seconds away from plunging his finger inside her when he stopped, slowed his kisses, and withdrew just long enough to render her completely naked. "Gorgeous," he murmured as he tossed the remainder of her clothes. "Absolutely gorgeous."

"Yes, you are." Her words barely formed around her ragged breaths. "Now where were we?"

"Breaking the coffee table."

"Screw the table." She sat and grabbed him by the waistband, then hauled him back to the bed and on top of her. He caught himself and limited their physical contact to his mouth on her nipple, right where he'd left off. She hissed her pleasure and fisted the comforter, yanking it out of sorts to reveal…Star Wars sheets? This would be a first.

"I'd rather screw you," he said, his tongue working her tight little nipple as he spoke.

"Then do it."

Oh, hell yes. "Are you sure?"

"Where ya been, green eyes? I told you I was drenched a long time ago. Also, I would have wounded you before I let you take off my pants."

"Good to know." He loved that she was threatening to kick his ass even as she tore at the linens and spread her legs beneath him. And there was just one layer of denim between him and…he dropped his head. "Crap."

"What?"

He sat back and calculated the distance to the nearest drug store. Too far. They'd both have plenty of time to come to their senses, and just this once, he didn't want to be sensible. Mentally he scavenged his apartment and came up empty, which only left one option. "I don't suppose you have any condoms?"

She pushed up to her elbows and stared. "You're kidding, right?"

He tried not to notice her breasts, but they were spectacular. And teetering on off limits. "What about your brother? Does he have any around here?"

"Okay, first of all, ew. Second, he has no game whatsoever. There's no way he owns condoms."

As she spoke, Crosby reached past her and rummaged through the drawer in the table by the bed. He extracted a strip of condoms. "Bingo."

She fell back to the mattress and closed her eyes. "Oh, God. And the box was open?"

"The box was open," Crosby confirmed. But Estelle had him worried. And there *were* Star Wars sheets on the bed. He looked more closely at one of the packets. "They're not expired. Over three years left."

"Seriously, ew. He's got to be making balloon animals with those things."

"As a red-blooded man who has been single forever, I can assure you that's not what they're there for. If nothing else, it's optimism." He dropped the packet on the table and dove back in. He was well into a long, lazy tour of her mouth when he realized she'd managed to work loose the button of his jeans. He had a brief come-to-Jesus moment when she snatched down the zipper, but he was rather uncomfortably lodged in the down position, which at least saved him from a run in with the metal teeth of hell.

Been there, done that, had the scar to prove it.

"You really should be naked with me," she murmured as she worked his jeans lower. They weren't going too far, though. Not unless he helped, which he didn't do in the least when he dipped his head to once again covet her nipple. He stayed only long enough to enjoy the victory of her gasp, then eased lower. He ran his tongue along the underside of her breast, right where it met her rib cage.

She threaded her fingers through his hair and arched beneath him, muttering "Oh, God. I didn't know that was a spot."

He ignored her, except for the smile that he hid against her skin, and continued his tour across her abdomen, leaving a trail of kisses. He reached to softly cup her breasts, to gently toy with their hardened peaks, as he made feather soft tracks past her belly button. A couple inches lower and he moved his hands to her waist, then to rest on her thighs, which were open. "Nice landscaping," he murmured, grinning when she let go of an exasperated breath. "Clearly a woman who knows her work."

"My *work* has nothing to do with that landscaping. Also, you're a tease."

"I'm not a tease. I'm savoring." Truth was, he was once again about to embarrass himself, but if that happened she'd probably never know it. He'd be hard as a rock again in no time, and his jeans were still damp from the water playground. Nice contingency plan, but screw that. He wanted her. *Yesterday*.

He lowered his head and blew gently on her swollen clit while she squirmed. He could only imagine the litany of profanity going through her head, but he wanted to hear it with his own ears. Determined to drive her wild, or at least to have her meet him there halfway, he gave her a long, slow lick…at the crease of her inner thigh.

"Damn you, Crosby."

He bit back laughter and moved to the other side. The painful throbbing in his jeans was almost more than he could take, but so wrapped up with pleasure that he didn't want it to end. But it would get a whole lot better before that happened.

He stopped his ministrations long enough to lose his pants, and the next time he put his tongue on her, it was a bull's-eye. She shrieked and grabbed his head as he plunged inside her, sucking and licking until he couldn't hold on any longer. Finally, dislodged by her hip action, he grabbed the condom. *Greater sensitivity*, the package read. *Just* what he needed. He tore open the wrapper, saying a silent thanks to Estelle's brother that would probably get his ass kicked, and rolled on the latex. A cool, tingly feeling greeted him.

Time to get hot.

He maneuvered to her opening and assumed the position. He glanced at her to make sure she was still on board and found her looking intently at him. Their eyes locked and stayed that way, making the moment he sank into her body one of the most intimate experiences of his life. The intensity startled him so much that he almost looked away, but he didn't. He couldn't.

He withdrew slightly, then pushed further inside, repeating until he was buried. Her fingernails dug into his biceps. "How do you like it? Easy"—he withdrew then slowly pumped back into her body—"or hard?" This time when he withdrew, he slammed back inside, holding back just enough so he didn't hurt her.

"Oh. My. God." Her eyes rolled back in her head and a smile tipped the corners of her mouth. He felt her squeezing him and nearly lost what was left of his sanity.

"How do you want it?" he asked again, grinding hard against her.

He rocked his hips, opening distance between them, and she whimpered at his absence. She whimpered harder when he thrust again. She reached up to grip the metal poles that comprised the headboard, causing her breasts to sit high and round on her rib cage. "Hard," she whispered.

She didn't need to tell him twice. He hooked her legs under his arms and drove into her, balls deep. He rocked against her, grinding hard against her clit, but before the scream fully left her lips, he was gone again. She took skin off his arms in her attempt to make him stay, but he left anyway, repeating the whole bump and grind at a punishing pace. The bed rocked, the metal frame slamming against the wall, Estelle coming undone. By some blessed miracle, he held on, but barely as her body trembled. When her cries softened, he took her mouth in a languid kiss — a slow exploration of tangled tongues and heavy breathing as he moved gently inside her, waiting for her to come back around.

He tasted her neck, finding and nipping the tender hollow behind her ear, then worked his way down to suck on her breast. He loved her responsiveness. Loved the feel of her hard nipple stabbing his tongue, reaching for him. Straining. *Begging*. He took as much in his mouth as he could, rasping his tongue back and forth as he continued to rock his hips. She was so soft inside. So hot. So every damned cliché you ever heard, but so much more. She had him wound tight, strung out, and barely holding on, and he loved it. Had never known anything like it. The more he paced himself, the more dizzied he felt. His entire body craved release. Demanded he plow into her. But she whispered soft sighs and breathed contentment. She wasn't ready…not until she could scarcely breathe at all.

He reached between them, feeling blindly for her clit as he switched sides, leaving one breast wet to the cool air while burying the other stiff, needy peak under his mouth. When his fingers hit pay dirt, she jolted and arched beneath him, nearly knocking him to the side. And giving him a hell of an idea.

He rolled over, taking her with him without breaking a single point of contact, then reluctantly relinquished his hold on her breast so she could straighten. She straddled him, fully impaled, and with a cat-that-ate-the-canary grin, started riding him at such a coy, measured speed that he just knew she was fucking with him.

"You think you can do that to me," she said, "and expect me to take over up here?"

"That's kind of my point," he argued. Probably against his best interest. "I did that to you. Figured I earned a moment of respite."

"If you want respite, I can just…" She moved one leg like she was headed for a dismount.

He closed his hands on her legs and locked her down. *Nope.* "You can just ride me," he ordered. "*Hard.*"

She flattened her hands on his abdomen, then traced a fingertip across his chest. And made no move whatsoever toward speed. He kicked up his hips a little, nudging up the momentum.

She smiled, all smoky blue eyes and flushed skin, as she sweetly braced herself and foiled his efforts. Her blonde, sweat-darkened hair hung in soft waves.

"You look amazing," he said. "Especially like this."

"Just like this? Because I thought you wanted a little more action." She increased her speed just a little, but it was a Richter scale kind of difference, with each uptick of intensity measuring ten times the one before it.

He moved his hands to her hips and plied her into the fast lane. "Until it cripples you," he said.

"Charming."

"Will be," he sputtered. Because she'd kicked it into overdrive, sliding back and forth in short bursts, grinding against him, driving him hard from every angle at once. The explosive friction between their bodies made an unbearable contrast to her heat. He was buried, balls deep, in an inferno. She was wet, her skin hot and slick, her hair flinging all over the place while she worked him like she had a road map to his fucking soul.

The edges of his vision darkened, and for a brief moment, he wondered if the sun had imploded. Then he realized it was him. Radio static crackled in his ears. He was somehow numb and at once blissfully aware of the pleasure that roared through him while he involuntary jerked like a fire hose. He prayed the latex would hold under the force of his orgasm. Prayed he'd *survive*. And considering her inevitable departure, prayed he was wrong about what she'd done to him.

Ruined.

Even though he knew damn well it was the truth.

And he wouldn't trade it for anything.

Chapter Nine

Estelle woke in the middle of the night to the sublime feeling of being the little spoon, all enveloped in the heat that was Crosby. But the heat stopped there. The room was *frigid*. Skiing-in-Tahoe frigid.

"Crosby." The stage whisper didn't rouse him, so she jabbed backward with her elbow. "Crosby!"

"*Ow*," he muttered through sleep. "What?"

"It's freezing in here." She tugged uselessly at the comforter that was twisted beneath them.

"I feel nothing but heat."

"You're going to feel my elbow again if you don't let go so I can go turn that thing off."

He released her, but before she could get up he climbed over her and punched one of the buttons about ten times. "It occurs to me I forgot the remote."

"It has a remote?" Like she cared. She was too busy staring at him. Naked. Utterly naked. Could *not* have been more delectable if he'd been carved from cheesecake. Or maybe chocolate. Chocolate and wine and—

"Would have been handy, no?" He reached to grab his jeans from the floor and pulled them on. Then he found and tossed her his T-shirt.

"Clothes?" She was no expert, but she was pretty sure his bones had melted right alongside hers. The fact that he was opting to cover the fun parts didn't bode well to that point.

"Just so I can tear it off you later," he said. "I want to show you something outside while we defrost."

She pulled on the shirt and lived a few lifetimes in the way he watched her as she moved toward him. When she shivered, she wasn't sure if it was him or the cold. "I don't think you can see anything through that nasty glass."

"Don't need to." He unlocked the window and slid it open, then stepped outside onto the fire escape and turned to offer her his hand. "It's nice and warm out here."

Her hesitance evaporated. "Sold. But if that cat shows up and shuts the window, I'm moving out."

"If the cat shuts the window, you won't have to. You'll *be* out."

"Funny." She straightened and cast an uneasy look toward the ground a good thirty feet below. "What are we doing?"

"C'mere." He leaned against the building and held out his arms. He didn't have to ask twice. Even before they'd had sex, she'd loved the strength of his arms. She had no business relishing their protection, but no woman alive could resist that kind of warmth. When he wasn't blowing her mind with carnal exploits, he made her feel adored. Cherished. And while Estelle had never before had a one-night stand, she'd been in a relationship or two that left her feeling a hell of a lot more empty after sex than did this relative stranger.

She nestled back against him, enjoying the easy way his arms fit around her.

"What do you see?" he asked.

She looked down. Way down. And hoped no one was looking up. "An alley. Hopefully an empty one, considering my lack of undergarments. Although I think that might a homeless guy over there." She pointed to a still form near the corner of the building. "Unless he's dead."

"That's a garbage bag. You really don't like the city, do you?"

"It's dirty. It's crowded. There's no space. No sky."

"Look up."

She did as he asked. Murky gray stared back, a shadow that never seemed to end. Mottling suggested clouds interceded in the distance, but overhead a single point of light attempted to break through. "I see the sky. Maybe a star."

"Probably a planet. We kind of suck at stars here."

"Is this supposed to help your case?"

He leaned down and nuzzled her ear. "Stay with me, Estelle," he said with a soft laugh. "What else do you see?"

He was doing something to her ear that made heat pool low in her belly. She was still tender. Still primed. Still needy—not because he hadn't satisfied her, but because he'd done it a little too well. She felt a bit drunk, and the dim ambient lighting did nothing to kill the mood. "Tall buildings with ridiculous electric bills," she managed. "And employees who don't know how to turn off the lights."

"Probably cleaning crews. All those lights out there. All

those people, they all have a story. It's not green, I'll give you that. But it's humanity. People hanging out. Hanging on. Some fight for survival. Others fight for more. But this whole damned place is full of life."

His passion left her taken aback. "You really love it here, don't you?"

"I do." His words were soft. Reverent, almost. "My grandfather founded Fusion Air in 1939, training my father and then me in the business. When I look out there, I see possibilities. I wonder what he must have thought seventy-five years ago when he decided to make a go of it, or what he'd think of us now. That man single-handedly started something that has given purpose to three generations."

"That's an incredible responsibility."

"Crushing sometimes," he admitted. "Pretty well ties you down. Especially as the oldest son."

"Did you ever want to do anything else?"

"I was never unhappy doing this, especially with all the time it gave me with my grandfather. He taught me every-thing he knew. I swear that man had the patience of a saint, but he wanted me to carry on his life's work, and I've always been honored to do that for him." His laugh reverberated through her. "I mean, hell. Look where it got me today."

She was glad he couldn't see the stupid grin she knew stretched her face. "I thought we blamed that on your shopping cart maneuvering skills."

"Nah. That didn't get me into your apartment."

"It would have."

"Good to know."

"So you can't go. And I can't stay," she murmured.

They both grew quiet, unable to come up with a way to

get over that impasse between them. In the end, he broke the silence, his voice resonating close to her ear, drawing chills to her flesh. "You still cold?"

"No."

He flattened his palms on her belly, dragging the shirt up, exposing her lady bits to the night air. Despite the fact that she was four floors up on a rusty fire escape overlooking a filthy concrete hell, pinpoints of desire studded her vison, filling the night sky with tiny bursts of light. Heat flooded her V-zone. She needed his touch, but he denied her. Work-roughened hands edged higher, palming her breasts. They ached, the tips sore but begging anyway. He refused all but the slightest brush of his calloused fingertips. "When you think of this city you hate so much," he murmured, his lips brushing her ear. "Think of this."

He released one breast, sliding his fingertips down her side, tracing the curve of her waist and the flare of her hips before settling between her legs. The slightest touch against her clit made her tremble, the height without solid ground dizzying her. "I can't hate anything when I think of this."

"That would be my point."

She playfully ground her butt against him. "That's not your only point."

He spun her with a growl. The murky, tepid darkness didn't dilute the intensity of his gaze. Or his eyes. Those damned eyes.

For a long *tense in a toe-curling kind of way* moment, neither of them moved. Then his mouth touched hers, and the sanctity of the kiss shook her to her core. He wound his fingers through her hair, his tongue tangling with hers. He stole her breath. Stole her heart. Made her want to love the city. It didn't matter that she'd known him less than two days. She just wanted this feeling, over and over again.

But it would end.

She nearly sobbed at the thought. Then he slipped his fingers deep inside her, immediately finding and stroking her G-spot, and she almost sobbed at *that*. She whimpered and clutched his shoulders, but he didn't relent. He circled her clit with this thumb, not quite hitting the sweet spot but not giving her any breathing room, either, and she clamored for a way to wrap herself around him. She wanted him between her thighs—not just his very talented fingers, but all of him. She wanted to ride him.

Again.

As if he'd read her growing urgency, he maneuvered so she had her back to the ladder that stretched skyward. Unlike the staircase type that stretched from floor to floor, this was just a flat, stationary set of rungs that went to the roof. She grabbed onto the metal and held on for dear life as his fingers explored her. Weakened her. When she lost the warmth of his touch, she peered through half-lidded eyes to see him opening his jeans. He didn't take them off. Just shoved them down enough to work himself free, then dug in his pocket.

"When did you put that in there?" she asked when he came up with a condom, which he immediately tore into.

"Earlier, while your eyes were rolled back in your head." He punctuated the words with a boyish grin, then sheathed himself while she stared hungrily. She had no idea how he fit inside her, let alone so perfectly. She needed to brush up on her anatomy, but right now she'd rather brush up on his.

"Hang on," he said, lifting her legs.

She gripped the rungs and watched, almost dumbstruck, as he entered her. *Stand up sex. On the fire escape.* "What if people are watching?"

"As the man buried inside you right now, I'd like to think you don't care. As a decent citizen, I can assure you we aren't any more interesting than a pair of shadows." He rocked his hips against her and whispered against her lips, "Very naughty shadows."

"My absolute favorite kind."

He reached around her on both sides and grasped the ladder while she gripped him with her legs. With the new angle, he pistoned deep. *Impossibly* deep. Her body clenched around him from the inside out. In the electrically-tingled fallout, she barely managed to hook her ankles around him before he rocked his hips, relenting the exquisite pressure only to drive back in, thicker, fuller, harder. She hung by her grip on the ladder, head thrown back between rungs, her body buoyed by his hips as he pumped dizzying waves of pleasure through her body with every thrust. Metal clanged and rattled a serenade to the tune of her being thoroughly fucked.

On a fire escape.

There was no build. No warning. Just wreckage. He sensed it, or she squeezed the holy mother out of him when she came, because his arms were around her, holding her, catching her before she could fall. As the world droned distantly around her, she had but one focus, and that was the thickness of him pulsing, buried to the hilt as he climaxed inside her. Everything else stilled, at least until he swayed. She held on as he staggered and made a grab for the ladder. Slowly, gravity shifted and settled around them. Once she no longer blinked a thousand pinpoints of light, she pulled herself up by the rungs.

"That's three," she managed. "Definitely number three."

He grinned, his gaze an inexplicable mashup of *world thoroughly rocked* and *Imma eat you alive*. Not-so-little Crosby swayed as he withdrew. Or maybe she swayed. Or maybe it was the damned rickety fire escape.

She was still staring at him, marveling over the thick, perfect arc, when he spoke.

"Come over Sunday," he said.

She blinked. "For sex?"

"No, for dinner. Actually, my mom's house. My parents' I mean."

"You want me to meet your mother?"

"And also to eat. She found out I was bringing the A/C over and wanted to know why."

"Did you tell her it was because I was drenched?"

"No. But my brother told her you were a woman, and that's pretty much all it takes."

She took a deep, unfocused breath. He wanted her to meet his family? Before gravity set in? "This happens often?"

"To my brothers. Not so much to me."

"I don't know. I'm not…I'm not going to be around long."

"All the more reason to say yes. It can be terrible, and that'll be okay because you're outta here, right?"

"You've got me there. I don't…" She saw the hopeful look in his eyes and melted. "Okay."

He perked. "Okay?"

"Yes, I'll go. But you'll put your pants back on before the main course, won't you?"

"Babe, as far as I'm concerned you *are* the main course."

"In that case, how about we go inside and work on dessert?"

"That sounds—"

The cat. The damned cat was on the windowsill.

Next to her, Crosby snorted.

"How is this even remotely funny?"

"It's just…I've never been cockblocked by a pus—"

He broke off as the cat broke his yellow devil glare to hop down into the apartment. A low growl rumbled in his wake.

Estelle elbowed Crosby in the ribs. "I rescued you once. This time is on you."

He glanced from her to the cat and back again. The cat snarled.

Crosby tucked himself in his jeans. "If that cat bites me again," he said, headed for the open window. "You're going to take a good, long look at my ass."

Estelle crossed her arms and watched as he tried to circle behind the cat. Another view of that ass?

She should be so lucky.

Chapter Ten

Estelle woke tangled in the sheets, the apartment at a perfectly sublime temperature for snuggling deep under the covers and making a day out of it. With the A/C cranked low—although not nearly as low as it had been earlier—she wasn't doing her part to resolve the energy crisis, but her sex-wrecked body welcomed every indulgence, no matter how small.

She rolled over and didn't see Crosby, but then she heard the shower. Thank God she'd scrubbed it down. Having him see that shower in its original state would be almost as embarassing as...*omigod*. The sex they'd had. The crazy part hadn't ended with the fire escape...it had *started* there. She had no idea she was such a freak, but now she knew...and she wasn't the only one. Hotty McHotterson knew it, too. How the *hell* was she going to look him in the eye? Granted, he'd participated, but...

Oh. God.

The bathroom door swung open. Crosby, shirtless, jeans unzipped and unbuttoned, emerged in a burst of steam. Catching her stare, he offered an easy smile. "I hope you don't mind I used your shower. I tried asking, but you were dead to the world, and I didn't want to go to my apartment and disappear on you."

She watched the fine mist that dusted him merge into water droplets, which tip-toed down his ripped chest and stone-carved abs like they relished the ride. Why the hell wouldn't they? *She* had, and she'd bet the neighbors all knew it.

Oh. God.

He must think she was some kind of sex ninja. So much for friends only. That theory had been blown to hell, and she had never, ever let loose like she had with him. She was mortified. She sat up, dragging the sheet up with her to hide her nakedness, but trying not to be obvious about it.

His face froze with concern. "You okay?"

"Um, yeah. I just…have a thing." She felt around for her clothes.

"You have a thing?"

"A friend," she lied. Or maybe not. She'd have to call Peyton, her best friend from college. She was due to touch down that morning to visit her parents at their Hamptons estate after yet another stint in London or Paris or some other European stalwart likewise made of stone, and she *had* insisted they meet up. "Don't you have to go to work?"

"My first service isn't for about two hours. Do you want to get some breakfast? There's a place around the corner with the best glazed donuts on the planet."

Glazed donuts. Her favorite. *Of course.* Not as earth-shattering as the green pizza topping combo, but still. Was this guy anything close to real? He looked normal enough—if ripped sex gods were everyday things, and they *weren't*—but the way he moved inside her, like he could read her every desire, was almost disturbing. It was amazing and terrifying and it was bliss and insanity and…too much.

It was *too much*.

Finally, she found her tank top and yanked it on. Her shorts. He'd pulled them off and…that was, what, six orgasms ago? She peered over the side of the bed and found them in a ball, tangled with her underwear. She grabbed them both and maneuvered them on, as much under the covers as possible.

Crosby gave her an odd, puzzled look as she tried to finger comb her hair and failed. Great. He was probably thinking about the *thing* with the *thing* and… "I have to run," she said.

"Like, go running?"

"No. Just go." She grabbed her purse and her phone, which was down to a whopping ten percent battery after she'd failed to charge it—a side effect of getting fucked ten ways to Tuesday, she guessed—and pasted on her best everything-is-fine-as-long-as-you-ignore-whatever-is-going-on-right-now smile. "Can you lock up when you leave?"

She didn't wait for his reply. Of course he'd lock up. He was a freaking Boy Scout. Outside of the bedroom, anyway. Inside, he was a god. A legend. A sex machine.

Definitely not a Boy Scout.

She threw a wave over her shoulder as she fled in yesterday's clothes, her hair a wreck, and her flip flops on the wrong feet. Classic walk of shame with the added embarrassment of running from her own damned apartment.

And the best sex of her life.

But for what? She was leaving. *So* leaving.

Hands shaking, she used her last ten percent of phone charge to text Peyton.

Crosby flinched over Sawyer's incredulity. "*You* had sex?"

"Careful. I'm not sure the whole family heard." Their younger brothers, Ethan and Liam, were off on service calls, but both parents were in the front office. And while Crosby was looking for a shipment of parts, his brother was standing over him like he hadn't a care in the world. "And the sex wasn't the point. She *left*."

"She left her own apartment?" Sawyer asked as Crosby pushed past him.

He threw a couple of empty boxes to the side and unearthed a folder of blank estimates that should have been on one of the trucks. "Not only did she leave it, but she did so in yesterday's clothes. And I think her shoes were on the wrong feet."

Sawyer's expression was some mixture of awe and disbelief. "What the hell did you do to her?"

Crosby tried not to glare. He really did. But his brother's amusement at his expense merged with his frustration over Estelle to form a combustible force. Frankly, he was surprised he didn't incinerate Sawyer on the spot. "I hoped you'd have an idea," Crosby said, "seeing as how you can't keep your dick in your pants for more than five minutes."

Sawyer shook his head and laughed. "Yeah, but I can't

say I've ever made a woman *run*."

"It was more of a fast walk," Crosby muttered. Although that was a technical point at best. Gone was gone. "Don't you have work to do? Or is leaving me to do your work, along with my own, your way of admitting I'm twice the man you are?"

Sawyer leaned against the wall. "I stand corrected—on the running, I mean. Not the rest. And I repeat, what the hell did you do to her?"

He blew out a breath. So much for sparing the play by play, although there was no way there would be sex details. Not ever. Sawyer didn't need that kind of ammo, but more than that, Estelle deserved Crosby's respect. "I assaulted her with broken glass and pickle juice in the grocery store, then I brought her the A/C unit. We went to the park. We had pizza. She likes my pizza, you know."

"That green shit? Find her."

"Funny. Anyway, she asked to see my ass about fifteen times—"

"You made her ask more than once?"

Crosby picked up a box of tools, and the bottom fell out. A few choice words followed the clamor of forged steel hitting the concrete. He kicked the pile, scattering it. "The neighbor's cat bit me. She wanted to play nurse."

Sawyer's brow spiked skyward. "Again, you made her ask more than once?"

Crosby ignored him. "And she said she wanted to have sex, so it's not like I misread her."

"So you had sex once? And she didn't leave until morning?"

"We had sex until we ran out of condoms. We slept. She

woke up and split."

"Ah. Morning-after regrets."

Crosby frowned. "It wasn't like that."

Sawyer detached from the wall and helped with picking up tools. "It was clearly like that. And I know you don't get around all that much, but a box of condoms is supposed to last more than a night."

"It wasn't a full box. Why the hell would she take off like that?"

"Because she saw you in broad daylight, that's why. Take a good long look in the mirror, bro. But brace yourself first."

"You really aren't helping."

Sawyer dropped the handful of tools he'd picked up after the spill and turned his full attention on Crosby. "Look, man. You could have been the most amazing sex she ever had. You could have thoroughly rocked her world. You could have ruined her for every other man for life. None of that negates what morning light shines on sex between strangers. And I'm going to be straight with you, Crosby. You're one strange bastard."

"But—" *But what*? Forty-eight hours ago, he hadn't known her name. He couldn't reconcile that in his head. Two days. One incredible night. He felt like he'd known her forever. He certainly knew her body, but that didn't make much of an argument. Certainly nothing he'd lead with.

"Did you call her?" Sawyer asked.

"Not yet. I figured I'd give her some time."

"Good for you. Just don't wait too long, or she'll think you got what you wanted and hit the bricks."

"*She* left. *Her* apartment. Before I did."

Sawyer grinned. "Doesn't matter, bro. It's on you to

make it right."

Great. Absolutely no pressure there. Only there shouldn't have been. She wasn't going to stick around. He had a legacy to resurrect and no time for a social life until he did.

Maybe all she wanted was a one-night stand. Or maybe that was all she expected. Sure, she'd agreed to attend the family thing, but he'd kind of sprung that on her in a weak moment. But if they still had a chance—even one destined to last less than two weeks—he wanted it.

And he knew just what to do next.

Chapter Eleven

That afternoon, in a show of astounding competence, Estelle managed to find the restaurant suggested by her longtime bestie. Doing so required not just boarding the subway, but switching trains. She felt a little like a ferret in the tunnels, but when she emerged onto the street, and then minutes later found herself staring at the upscale eatery, she had to suppress the urge to do a victory dance.

Peyton Wentworth was a gorgeous twenty-eight-year-old socialite who routinely rubbed elbows with the upper crust on two continents. She was confident, stylish, and not someone who would ever run out of her own apartment wearing yesterday's underwear and the not-so-subtle scent of sex. But, as would any best friend, she'd absolutely appreciate that Estelle had.

They small-talked their way through the menu perusal. Paris was beautiful, Venice must-see. Whatever. Venice didn't even have grassy medians. Not unless seaweed counted, and

Estelle wasn't even sure they had that.

As soon as the waitress left with their orders, Peyton rested her arms on the table and fixed her stare on Estelle. "I know you don't care about Europe, so clearly you're stalling. Spill."

Estelle cut to the chase. "I had sex. All night."

One of Peyton's sculpted eyebrows lifted. "Did you say *all* night? Does he have a brother?"

"Three brothers. And I bailed on him this morning. Totally fled. It was embarrassing."

Peyton took a calculated sip of her wine. "The sex or the fleeing?"

"The sex was amazing. It was also…wild. I did things I've never done before. I said things I've never said before. I made *demands*. It was so easy and natural at the time, but then we ran out of condoms and slept, and when I woke, he was in the shower, and it was just…normal. And I just kind of freaked. Seriously, we did it everywhere. The bed. On the fire escape. And on the counter. And against the wall. And there may or may not be a handprint on my ass."

"Well, hot damn. And what's wrong with normal? Although, what you've described sounds anything but normal." Estelle must have blanched because Peyton quickly lay a hand on her arm. "Not like that. I mean, it sounds unbelievable. Pretty much every single woman alive dreams of what you've just described."

"Good for every single woman alive. Meanwhile? I. Am. Mortified."

"*Why*?"

"Because the neighbors probably heard me screaming like cheap porn, and, well, I know he did."

"I bet he loved it."

Estelle's face heated. "He definitely loved it…but that's not me. He didn't have me. He had some closet sex freak."

"That's *clearly* you." Peyton gave a dainty, socially acceptable snort. "Besides, it's a vacation thing. Be a freak… who is ever going to know?"

"You mean besides the neighbors?"

"They aren't *your* neighbors."

It was Estelle's turn to sit back in surprise. It finally hit her that Peyton wasn't being the voice of reason—at least not the way Estelle expected. "I had no idea you were so… unrefined."

Peyton laughed. "I'm so over refinement. I would *love* to have a wild night. Or even a mildly stimulating date."

"*You* can't get a date?"

Peyton waved off the question with one perfectly manicured hand. "We're here to talk about you. What did you do after you ran out on him?"

"I hid in the laundry room until I saw him leave." Estelle buried her face in her hands, not caring that her elbows sat uncouthly on the table. "The things I said. I can't even repeat them now."

"Were you drunk?"

"Stone sober. I can't decide if that makes it better or worse."

Peyton shrugged, but the sparkle in her eyes belied her indifference. "Maybe you just needed the right guy. Maybe he's *the one*."

"I've known him two days. He's married to the city, and I can't wait to get home. He's definitely not the one."

"Maybe he's the one for now."

"Is that a thing?"

"Look. You had some amazing sex, and you have, what, two weeks in the city?"

Estelle nodded.

"Then chill out. Have fun. Make it unforgettable. It may be temporary, but clearly you have stellar chemistry. What's so wrong with riding it out? Pun intended."

"Okay, so I spend my remaining week and a half as a freak. Just like that? If he's still talking to me, that is."

Peyton patted her arm. "I don't care if you went out the window on knotted sheets. Trust me, if there's a handprint on your ass, he's still interested."

The words haunted Estelle long after she and Peyton parted ways, but that wasn't all she took with her. Something was different about her friend. Peyton had never been one to brag, but during lunch she'd waved off her European adventure like it had been a boring trip to the grocery store—one devoid of broken pickle jars and spilled nuts—and hadn't mentioned a guy at all, other than to hint she could use a good one. And Estelle had really counted on being told she was crazy, and that she needed to cross her legs and get the hell off the fire escape before she was arrested. Instead she was…encouraged. Which meant the world had more or less slipped off its axis…likely about the time the whole fire escape started rocking. She and Crosby probably loosened those rusty old bolts in the aged, brittle masonry and would fall to their pornographic deaths if they tried it again.

If. Why was there even an *if*? Estelle shook her head. Peyton and Crosby were ganging up on her, and they didn't even know it. So she now knew she was a screamer. So the whole neighborhood did. What was the worst that could happen? Earl would smack her brother on the back—or the ankle, seeing as how the old man never seemed to get off the floor—and tell him she was a sex-yeller? By the time he got that tidbit secondhand, she'd be back home where all the sanity was. She'd deny the accusation, then hang up the phone and laugh. Or cry. Because Crosby made her scream for a reason, and to say she'd miss it when she left was an understatement of titanic proportion. She could not imagine a day when she wouldn't crave what he'd done to her, much less a moment when she'd let anyone else close enough to rival it.

She. Wanted. Crosby.

Which made her exodus seem pretty stupid. Most men avoided drama like the plague, and she'd stirred up a mess of it by fleeing. He hadn't called or texted, which meant he'd probably written her off. She wondered if she was still committed to meeting his family, then decided she maybe sort of hoped she was. If she could look him in the eye without dying of embarrassment or flinging her clothes to the ground, there was a chance they could move past her awkward destruction of the morning after glow.

Right?

Sigh.

Estelle managed to find her way back home, subway train switch and all, and was grateful to see she wouldn't have to climb over Earl to get to the stairs. Of course the elevator was still out, and frankly, Estelle wasn't sure she wanted to get on the thing. If nothing else, she should have great legs by the time her stint in New York was over.

On the second floor landing, her cell rang. Her heart leapt, and she immediately hoped for Crosby, but what she got was the picky client who was more worried about having her plants lined in military precision than she was the land-scape itself. Estelle wanted to ignore the call, but she'd have to deal with the woman sooner or later. Besides, wasn't that what she wanted? To get back to her life?

Still, she cringed inwardly as she accepted the call. "Hel—"

"Did you fix the design?" the woman interrupted. "My daughter's wedding is six months from today. I want every-thing to be perfect."

Estelle rolled her eyes. If the woman's daughter's wed-ding was perfect, no one would notice the symmetry, or lack thereof, of the trees. Besides, it was an indoor event. "Your design will be symmetrical," she promised. Several minutes later, she ended the call. It'd be difficult to appease the wom-an. Though part of her thrived on the challenge, and all of her enjoyed designing wedding landscapes, she had to admit that high-maintenance clients were her least favorite part of a job she otherwise loved. Estelle had been thrilled for the high-profile exposure potential, but the woman's irrational demands were just…ugly.

Uglier even than New York City.

And yet another reason she should be home, not here.

When she reached her floor, she opened the door from the stairwell to the hallway and froze. A beautiful six-foot-tall lace leaf maple tree was parked outside her apartment door, its root ball encased in a burlap sack. A card hung by a looped ribbon. She extracted it from the envelope.

Didn't think you'd see too many fire escapes back home. Thought instead you should think of me when you saw trees.

Oh, *melt.* It was by far the most ridiculous gift she'd ever received. And also the sweetest. She stood there for the lon-gest time just staring before she finally she let herself into the apartment and dragged in the tree. Her heart fluttered in a way that had absolutely nothing to do with four flights of stairs in triple-degree heat. Crosby was unreal. Maybe *that* was what should scare her. It probably would if not for the terrible injustice that rolled out in front of her, like a red carpet to hell.

She was leaving.

He wasn't.

Enjoy it while it lasts.

And then what? Be wrecked for life?

She positioned the maple by the window where she had a great view of it *and* the fire escape, then grabbed her phone and pulled up Crosby's number to text him.

Hardwood, huh? Freud would love this.

She hit send and tossed her phone on the sofa, then poured a glass of wine. It was her third. More points for the city…she could actually have a drink while she was out and not worry about getting home. She and Peyton had gone through three courses, so the buzz never happened, but there was nothing stopping her now.

She glanced at the bed. And against her will, she remembered her brother had had condoms. A partial pack. One she'd obliterated. With a man who gave her a tree.

Somewhat reluctantly, she grabbed her laptop off the coffee table and hit up Amazon for a refill and a new set of sheets. Blue and tan stripes. Nice and manly. Her brother was a decent guy. A bit of a *geek meets smart ass*, but if she could manage for one second to unsee his condom stash, she'd have to admit he was good-looking. He just needed to work on the presentation a little. Like losing the Star Wars sheets. She ordered the new set and, *shudder*, a replacement box of condoms, then closed the computer and drained the glass of wine. She eyeballed the fifty-inch flat-screen TV on the opposite wall and thought hard about queuing up something on Netflix. But instead she picked up a piece of junk mail laying on the coffee table and sketched a tiny container garden. One sized just right for the fire escape.

Her phone dinged.

Screw Freud. :) What does Estelle think?

She grinned. The man had used a freaking emoticon.

It's big and hard and only going to get bigger and harder. What's not to like?

I don't know. I kind of prefer warm and soft and wet.

Her grin grew until her face hurt. Before she could reply, he sent her another one.

I love it when you ride me. When you scream my name. When you want it so bad the whole building hears you beg.

If he kept that up, they were going to hear her beg some more. She picked up her wine and tried to get the last drops from the empty glass.

I love that you text with entire words, she wrote. She was joking, but not really. She was just sorely in need of a change of subject, or she'd have to add a vibrator to that order. Sheets, condoms, and a vibrator…a guy in a warehouse somewhere would have a blast packing that box.

She expected a text, so when the phone rang, she nearly dropped it. *Crosby*. Seriously? Suggestive texts were one thing. Actual speech? He *had* to be kidding.

But he *had* sent her a tree.

She answered and tried hard not to sound terrified. "Hey, you."

"That's what you love? Really?"

She laughed. His playful incredulity set her at immediate ease. What was she worried about? He melted her. The only reason she wouldn't be able to look him in the eye is because hers were rolled back in her head. That, or she was a couple thousand miles away. *Ouch*. "I was just getting warmed up."

"Good. Get yourself nice and warm. Get *hot*. Because I want to see you tonight."

"What if I want to wait and let you get me there?"

"No pants," he said. "When I get there, you're going to spread your legs for me, and I'm going to suck on your clit until you scream. And I'm not touching any other part of you until you do."

Her breath caught. Her nipples tightened, already protesting the idea of being ignored for the thirty seconds it would take her to fall apart with his teeth and tongue working her. So much for embarrassment. She had a feeling she'd hit a land speed record with the force of the orgasm he promised.

"Just in case we're not clear," he said, "I want you all the time. Long and hard and fast. Slow and easy. Floor. Fire escape."

"Not a one-night stand," she said, more to herself than him.

"No," he said softly. "Two amazing weeks, however you want them."

Chapter Twelve

Sunday, when Crosby picked her up to take her to his mother's dinner, Estelle was surprised to find his late-model pickup to be immaculate. Work trucks were supposed to be a wreck, weren't they? She tried to keep hers back home clean, but inevitably, the small gardening tools would pile up on the passenger-side floorboard alongside her gloves, and dozens of hand-drawn garden plans would litter the seat. She had software that allowed her to show clients their redesigned landscape in full color against an image of their homes, like a photograph into the future, but she saved that for the presentation. She preferred to think with a pencil in her hand.

After a fifteen-minute ride away from the heart of the city, Crosby parked the truck at a neatly maintained brick home with a small, albeit meticulously landscaped, lawn. "You and my mom," he said. "You have something in common."

"This is beautiful." Stunning, and not just because it was

beautiful, but because it was unexpected. "Your mother did this?"

"I thought you'd appreciate it."

Estelle swallowed whatever foreign feeling threatened her. *Just dinner.* With an entire family. Something she hadn't done in the whole of her dating life was now occurring following a couple of nights of crazy sex with a man who she'd gotten naked with after just a few hours. She didn't do random sex with strangers, so she had nothing with which to compare, but that all-nighter didn't feel cheap. *She* hadn't felt cheap. She felt…treasured.

"So the whole family will be here?" Temporary or not, that brought on the pressure.

"Every one of them. And they are all going to be studying your every move. I don't typically bring anyone to the family dinners, so I'd be surprised if they didn't try to wedge you under a microscope."

"That's comforting."

"Blame me. I won't talk, and it's driving them all crazy." He shrugged and tossed a sheepish smile her way. "We're typical men…we don't really open up unless we have to."

The front door opened, and a tall man with the same blonde hair as Crosby, streaked with the same natural lowlights, emerged to lean against the porch railing. "That's Sawyer."

"You sound worried."

"He's smiling. Never trust him when he smiles." With that, Crosby adopted a ridiculously dubious look and climbed out of the truck. He circled around and opened her door, and she let him, mainly because the enormity of this thing hit her hard. Again. *Meeting the family.* Was she crazy?

Crosby had three brothers…she knew how much trouble her *one* had caused her over the years. And considering Crosby didn't date, she might as well be walking into a pit of piranhas. If piranhas lived in pits.

She hopped from the truck and shivered when Crosby put his hand on the small of her back.

Sawyer opened his mouth, but Crosby cut him off. "Don't even."

"What?"

"Your face."

"It's the only one I've got." He turned his own set of laser-green eyes on Estelle. "Miss Donovan, I have no idea what you're doing with my brother, but it's a pleasure to meet you."

"Estelle, Sawyer," Crosby said by way of introduction. "And I'd like to apologize in advance for his mere existence."

Before she could do more than smile, an older woman joined them on the porch. She had her sons' coloring, though she was a good foot shorter than either of them, and a softer, youthful face that had Estelle second-guessing whether she was old enough to be Crosby's mom. "You must be Estelle," she said warmly.

The voice from the phone. It seemed a lifetime ago that Estelle had called Fusion over the dead air conditioner. "It's so nice to meet you, Mrs. Chase. I can't tell you how much I appreciate your generosity with the spare air conditioner. Crosby won't tell me how much I owe, but I'd love to com-pensate him."

"In his defense," Sawyer said with a snicker, "there are some services for which a man just doesn't want compensation."

Crosby's mom offered a gracious smile, holding it even

as she playfully smacked Sawyer in the back of the head. "Call me Alice," she said. "And come on in. You might as well meet the rest of these holy terrors. Are you an only child?"

Estelle followed her, trailed by Crosby and Sawyer, into a spacious, open floor plan—a clearly modern renovation that maintain much of the home's original integrity, with tall baseboards and a fireplace made of old red brick, the edges softened by time. "No, I have a brother."

"My condolences, dear." She gestured toward a large, L-shaped leather sofa that held three carbon copies of Crosby and Sawyer, each of whom stood to greet her. "Estelle, meet, Liam, Ethan, and Russell. You can blame the elder statesman of the group for the behavior of these boys."

"It's my good, strong genes," Russell said with a wink as he reached to clasp her hand.

"I've done my best to raise it out of them," Alice muttered, though humor glinted in her eyes. "For what good it did. Excuse me just a moment while I check dinner. Thank goodness you weren't here last week. Crosby was supposed to bring ingredients for dessert and couldn't find his way to the grocery store and back. These boys went stark raving mad without it."

Oh God. Totally her fault. Did they know?

"Because we love your baking," Liam said, as he and the others returned to their seats.

Alice waved a flustered hand and left for the kitchen.

"Did you hear that?" Ethan asked. He leaned back against the sofa cushions and rested his hands behind his head. "We were completely normal until Crosby didn't bring back the ingredients for dessert last week."

"Not that we blame him," Sawyer said.

Russell's brow climbed. He looked from Sawyer, who was smirking, to Crosby. "Why?" he asked. "What were you doing?"

Crosby shot Sawyer a warning glance, which he ignored with a gleeful smile. "Dumping pickle juice on Estelle."

"If that's a euphemism," Russell said, "I don't want to know what for."

Crosby rolled his eyes. "No, *Dad*. I actually broke a jar of pickles on her."

"Unconventional," Liam said. "But it clearly worked."

Sawyer snorted. "Damn straight."

Oh, God. Estelle wanted to crawl under the floorboards, but for the death glare Crosby fixed on his brothers. She felt oddly protected, the feeling unfamiliar, but good. Almost worth the embarrassment of having tidbits of her sex life flung from one side of the room to the other.

"Language!" Alice called from the kitchen.

Crosby took Estelle's hand and led her toward the back of the house. "I'm showing Estelle the garden."

Alice popped out of the kitchen. "Do you garden?"

"Actually, I'm a landscape architect. You've done a beautiful job on your front yard."

"Oh, honey, I'll have to borrow you one of these days. I volunteer with one of those neighborhood beautification groups, only we can't seem to stick to our own. There's nothing better than fixing up a tired old yard for someone who can't do it for themselves. Really brings them joy, and it lasts all season."

"That's such a wonderful thing to do," Estelle managed, more than a little taken aback. She was still reeling from the sight of the thriving greenery. That there was room for actual landscaping so close to the city's urban center floored her.

"Might be for selfish reasons," Alice said with a smile. "I think I get more out of it than they do. Anyway, you two get out there so you can get back. I'm putting the rolls in the oven now."

"Dinner smells delicious," Estelle said.

"You'll be blown away," Crosby told Estelle. "People beat down the door to get to her food."

"You boys would beat down the door to get to a bag of marshmallows. Makes me think I work too hard."

"We appreciate you," Crosby assured her.

"And marshmallows," came a voice from across the room.

Crosby took Estelle's hand and led her through the house, which was larger than it appeared from the outside. It shone from top to bottom, from the gleaming wood floors to the sparkling appliances. She'd always thought the houses near here were small and dirty, but she was wrong. Embarrassingly so. And, she realized, the stench was gone. Just minutes from the city, and aside from the small lots, she felt miles and miles away.

The back yard was lusher than the front. And the flowers…they were astounding. Brightly colored blooms burst from every direction, their hues beautifully complimenting and contrasting one another as they tumbled down trellises and from weighted stalks that teetered in the humid summer air. Straight out of a Disney movie, a pair of birds fluttered and preened in a stone birdbath situated in one corner. A tiny vegetable patch sat in the middle, its edges flowing with the surrounding flower beds to create a path that wound through the space, leading to a bench swing parked over a patio made from cobbled slate.

"This is unbelievable. Your mother did all of this?"

"Between doing and giving orders, yes. We haul in plants when she asks, but she loves to get her hands dirty."

"The neighbor outreach program idea is…beautiful." Estelle had heard of such things in sitcoms and the occasional news story, but she'd never been so close to it. She'd never seen the real people behind it.

"Yeah, it is. I've helped her with some of the grunt work. It's emotional for these people. Many are elderly. Some are wheelchair bound and couldn't do it if they wanted, and others are just too strapped for cash to plant anything in their yards. Hard to justify putting flowers and mulch in when you need every penny to keep the lights on and the fridge from being empty. It almost always brings them to tears. The men, too."

Estelle took a tentative step into the yard, wanting to be a part of it, as much as she worried she'd disturb the birds, which now numbered three. She couldn't think of a time when one of her clients had been brought to tears. The best she could hope for was payment at the end of the day, and rarely did that come with emotion. Not that her clients were rude, but they hired her to do a job, and she did it. Her mother's garden aside, Estelle's life's passion ended in a business transaction, and for the first time, she wondered if any of those people for whom she worked ever stopped to really *see* what she'd done. She wanted to know all about the program—what it entailed, who they chose to help…how *she* could help.

But she wouldn't be around for that, would she?

"Funny thing about all this nasty concrete," Crosby said, his quiet tone giving her the impression he read her mind. "People here see enough of it. They really appreciate the green stuff."

"Okay," she said. "You win. You've changed a major perception—or should I say misperception—I've held about the city. I would love to make people cry with my work."

"Ah, that makes four, does it not? And you have how many days left?"

"Six days." And they were officially flying. Because suddenly her work felt meaningless, she needed a change of subject. "But that doesn't explain the other thing."

"What other thing?"

"The thing where Sawyer knows so much about the *services* for which you chose not to be compensated."

He shrugged, a poor distraction from the boyish grin that lit his face. "I told you, we only talk when it's necessary."

"And what was so necessary about us?"

He grabbed her fingers and tugged her close. "We are beyond necessary. We're *essential*, at least for the next week. Which is why I had to stoop to asking my brother why you fled your own apartment the morning after. But that was all I told him."

"No details?"

"Are you kidding me? Do you think I want him looking at you knowing you can literally bend over backwards?" He leaned in and kissed her softly.

She melted to her toes. It wasn't fair. Even the kind of kiss that wouldn't be embarrassing should his family see them seemed to change her. Since she met Crosby, her world had been a series of shifts—some subtle, some seismic—and it was becoming more and more clear to her that it didn't matter if this thing lasted two days or two weeks or two years…he'd changed her. What they had together changed her. And like it or not, there was no going back to who she had been.

But there was no staying, either. Not in the city. Not when her whole life was on the opposite coast.

Wasn't it?

Crosby couldn't keep his eyes off Estelle. She wore a simple sundress, but she was so beautiful, he ached inside. His family loved her, which he'd expected, but he worried they'd overwhelm her. He hadn't wanted her to be uncomfortable, but he did want her to meet his mother and see that green did exist inside the city limits…that it mattered to the people there, too. But he needn't have worried for her comfort. By the time the group had polished off the last of his mother's three homemade pies, she was clearly at home.

He liked that a little too much.

Because in a week, she'd be gone.

"When does your brother come back?" he asked.

"Saturday. His flight comes in a few hours before mine leaves, so we're going to try to have a drink at the airport before we go our separate ways."

"What kind of writing does he do? I know you said technical, but I'm not sure what that entails."

"He writes instruction manuals and maintenance and operating guides with a goal of toning down the big words so they're user-friendly for the average person. Or at least that's what he told me."

"You think he'd be willing to do some work for Fusion? We hand out the manufacturer's instructions, but they're not exactly user-friendly. A rewrite in plain language would be fantastic."

"I'm sure he would." She frowned. "I still haven't broken the news to him about the air conditioner."

"Keep it," he said. "I have the old one on standby if for some reason he wants it back, but if not, we'll credit the trade in, and he can make payments on the new one. Or, rather, we'll get him one that fits the apartment. If he's not interested, he can just send it back for no charge. Just have him give me a call, and we'll work it out." They stopped in front of their building. After returning from his mom's, they'd walked to get some coffee. Now that whole awkward first meeting was happening all over again, one week to the day after the original. Only this time she didn't smell of pickle juice, and he didn't have to wonder how incredible it would be to taste every inch of her body.

He knew.

But there was so much more he wanted to know. Like if she liked the beach. Or how she'd look in the winter, bundled up against the weather, cheeks pink and snowflakes snagging on those mile long lashes. He bet he could look into her eyes in the heart of a blizzard, and no matter how many clouds choked the horizon, he'd see a clear summer sky.

"I really like your family," she said, dragging him from his thoughts.

"Which makes you completely insane or..." *Don't finish that.*

"Or what?"

"Or maybe they're not bad in small doses." *Yeah, whatever.*

"I have a feeling Sawyer was really holding back."

He laughed. "I'm surprised he managed as well as he did, but you're right. Even at his worst, though, there are some lines even he won't cross."

"What about you?"

Her suddenly playful tone had him on edge. A very good edge. "What do you mean?"

She traced her fingertips down his chest. "Are there any lines you won't cross?"

He toyed with the hem of her dress, dragging it a precarious distance up her thigh. "Any particular lines you had in mind?"

She grabbed a fistful of his shirt and pulled him down for a kiss. "Why don't you come upstairs, and I'll tell you all about it?"

"You're going to *tell* me?"

"You have a better idea?"

"Sure do," he said, grabbing her and tossing her over his shoulder. She shrieked and giggled as he carried her into the building, saying hello to Earl on his way to the stairwell. Once they were alone, he set her down and pinned her to the wall, kissing every inch of exposed skin until she was gasping. Then he took her upstairs, and they crossed all kinds of lines together.

Except one.

The fucking state line.

The one line he just couldn't forget.

Chapter Thirteen

The week passed quickly. Crosby spent almost every night at Estelle's apartment, and each day he took her somewhere — not the touristy spots, but the places where real life happened. And but for the lack of fresh air, she loved it.

But she still loved home.

She had a gorgeous four-bedroom house on a quiet street with wonderful neighbors. She'd bought it as a fixer-upper and poured her heart into it. It was the perfect place to raise a family. The fact that she hadn't met anyone to share that dream hadn't deterred her…until now.

Now the only man she could see was Crosby.

Logic dictated the butterflies would wear off or fly away or whatever they did. That it was new and exciting, and it couldn't last. That if things were different and they stayed together, that eventually they'd settle into a routine that would kill the thrill. *Whatever.* What good did logic do when the idea of sharing a pizza was exciting? It wasn't like he was showing her the world. He was showing her *his* world, and she loved it. Every mundane, ordinary bit of it.

And it broke her heart.

Made her angry.

She was twenty-eight years old. She'd busted her butt building her life and her business. She had the responsibility and the honor of a memorial garden back home that her mother had planted with her own two hands. The fact that she even considered life somewhere else pissed her off. She didn't work that hard to build something from which she could walk away.

She *wouldn't*.

She and Crosby were at her apartment, sharing a bottle of wine on the fire escape. The city lights had a way of delaying sunset—something she'd grown to appreciate as her time there had grown short. Two more nights. Including that one.

Her chest hurt.

Crosby tightened his hand on hers. He had a way of reading her, of knowing when she needed him. She wondered how long that would last.

Two more nights.

His warm gaze was on hers. "Do you still hate the city?" he asked.

She looked up at him, the fading light glittering in her eyes. "No," she said. "But my life isn't here. I can't stay."

"I know," he said. "But maybe you'll visit?"

Emotion choked her throat. Either she hadn't had enough to drink or she'd had too much, because the heat that pricked her eyes had no business there. And that was when the reality of their situation really hit. Getting on a plane wouldn't make her forget a damned thing. How long would she sit in her big empty house and think of him? Or him with his family? If Grady accepted Crosby's job offer, even her brother would be a part of what she'd leave behind.

Visits. Sure. "I have more with you than I've ever had with anyone, which is pretty sad considering how long we've known each other. But we both know it's ending. Hanging on won't stop that from happening."

"I don't think it's sad. We connected. People do that."

"Yeah, but I don't know why I had to connect with someone on the wrong coast."

He shook his head. "Don't know, but that doesn't make the connection any less real. We can be friends, Estelle."

"Friends with benefits?"

"No. Yes. Dammit, I don't want to end this just because we don't live in the same place."

"So you'll do what? Wait for me? To come back once or twice a year?"

She hadn't been able to keep the edge out of her voice, and the hurt that flashed across Crosby's face tore through her. "I don't know. What's the right answer here? I sit around like a love struck fool because we had an amazing couple of weeks, and I can't see past that? Or I pretend that this small amount of time we've had together isn't better than anything I've ever had before and just move on like it never happened?"

"I can't answer that for you," she said.

A muscle in his jaw twitched. For a long moment he stared ahead, not appearing to focus on anything. By the time he turned to her, the air was thick in a way that had nothing to do with the humidity. "What do you *want*?"

She wanted things to be less complicated. She wanted an answer that felt right—not one that made them both miserable. But there wasn't any such thing. All they could do was move on, but if he wanted her blessing…screw that. She was hurting, too. "I'm sorry…are you actually asking me if I *want* you to bend some random woman over the fire escape and fuck her until the whole neighborhood knows your name? In the name of moving on? Forgetting me? New week, new girl?"

His green eyes turned stony. "Is that all you think this was?"

She blinked back the threat of tears. Of course that wasn't all it was. That's what made it so damned *hard*. Real feelings didn't happen this quickly. And even if they did, they weren't allowed. She wasn't going to do a long-distance relationship. And she wasn't going to be able to break things off with him if he kept looking at her like that.

Like what they had mattered. Like it could be more.

"Yes," she whispered. Her voice shook, and she prayed he wouldn't notice. That he'd just *go* so this didn't have to be any harder. Because she couldn't afford to fall. Not another inch. She straightened. Her voice strengthened. And she lied. "Sex. That's all it was."

Stone-cold silence fell like a brick between them and shattered, as if masonry was prone to such a thing. She braced herself for his anger, knowing she deserved it. Knowing the last thing *he* deserved was to be dismissed as random sex. But she couldn't stand to hold on. Not if it meant letting go in two short days.

"Kiss me," he said.

"What?"

"Kiss me. Kiss me, and tell me you don't feel anything. Tell me you don't want me to touch you. Tell me you won't spend the whole damned night wishing I was *fucking* you, and I'll go."

She wanted to bite out the words, but she couldn't force them from her throat. She couldn't look at this man and demean anything he was to her. "I…I can't."

"What does that tell you, Estelle?" His gaze tore over her. Decimated her.

Weakened her.

"Does it matter?" she managed. Dammit, she needed to breathe. That was what was so wrong with the city. No air. She'd said that all along, and that much would never change.

Fighting the pain that threatened to crush her, she dropped his hand and went back through the window into the apartment. She knew he'd follow, but there was something to be said for solid ground. And more wine. She had her hand on the bottle for a refill when he came back inside. His face looked as if it had been carved from stone. She froze when she realized the emotion behind that mask was because of her. It was *for* her.

For a long moment, they just stared at one another. She opened her mouth to say something, *anything* to break the tension, but he spoke first.

"You're damn right it matters." And then his mouth was on hers. It was the kind of kiss that belonged on a train platform in the pouring rain, but there was no platform. No rain. Just a small studio apartment with a broken elevator and a Hell Cat and a homeless man in the lobby. Nothing that should be perfect, but in some stupid, heartbreaking way, it was.

He was.

He lifted her onto the counter, knocking over her wine glass in the process. It hit the sink and shattered. That would be her. Like a speeding train into a brick wall. She could see it coming from a mile away.

"I'll replace it," he said, running his hands under her shirt. He managed to unsnap her bra, then just as quickly fit his hands over her breasts. They were heavy. Achy. She wondered if he could feel what he did to her, then she wondered if she did the same to him.

Too much. Too damn much.

The look in his eyes had been wild. Feral. Now, as he softly stroked her breasts, she saw something else. Something she wasn't sure she wanted to name.

She swallowed the pain and threw back his words, a biting question that did nothing to ease the pain of knowing how close they were to over. "Are you going to *fuck* me now?"

He shook his head. Soft. Slow. "No, Estelle, I'm not. I'm going to make love to you. I'm going to worship every inch of your body and treasure every moment you share it with me. And if you can walk away from that and forget, then you're stronger than I am."

He waited, eyes full of questions. Probably waiting for her to say no. But she couldn't speak, so she leaned in and kissed him.

And he her. In a thousand kisses, never like that. So slowly that time stood still. So deeply that he touched something new…something that had danced around the fringes of her conscious without allowing her to grasp it. Something that said too much about how she felt about him.

Something terrifying.

He scooped her from the counter and walked over to the bed. This time he didn't toss her down. He eased her to the mattress like she was fragile, then crawled over top of her. His weight and the heat of his body were exquisite. Solid. Warm. An anchor she never knew she needed. So she held on.

Held on until it hurt.

He spent several minutes undressing her, fulfilling his promise to kiss every inch, all the while avoiding her attempts to return the favor. When he finally shed his jeans, the sight of him nearly brought tears to her eyes. But that could wait, because he wasted no time rolling on a condom and sinking into her. His movements were slow, measured. All the feelings that usually came with flinging body parts and slapping skin had been reduced to earth-shattering precision. Every move, every inch resonated deep, and despite the slow burn between them, she was soon trembling, her skin sweat-dampened. She could only hold on, her fingers digging into his biceps or winding desperately through his hair, as he stretched her, filling her again and again. And not even the torturously slow motion could hold back the force of her orgasm. She felt its blinding impact from her head to her toes, from the blistering tension that seized her to the tenderness of the aftermath, where he kissed her gently, swearing under his breath as he climaxed, his own orgasm touching her in ways hers hadn't.

Because she knew it was good-bye.

They lay together for a long time afterward. He held her tightly from behind, no words between them. Just a darkened room, city lights taking the place of candles, in the very last corner in the world that was their own. She could tell by his breathing that he didn't sleep, and when a single tear rolled down her cheek, he brushed it away, though she hadn't thought it possible he'd seen it fall. The tender gesture made her choke back a sob she hadn't felt coming.

It wasn't fair, but no one ever promised it would be.

"Dammit, Estelle," he said, though his voice was soft. "What does that *tell* you?"

"It tells me this is too much. It can't happen like this."

He gently pulled against her shoulder until she lay on her back, facing him. "Well, guess what. It did. Do you really want to throw that away?"

"Throw *what* away? Whatever it is, it's temporary. We've known that from the beginning. Why are you trying so hard to define something that can't exist?"

"Because it *does* exist. And I don't know what to do with that, but I'm not going to turn my back and pretend it doesn't."

"What choice do we have?"

"What if we did have a choice? What if there were no miles between us?"

"What difference does it make?" This time, the tears fell in earnest. Silent, as if they, too, knew they didn't have any fight left. "I don't have an argument, Crosby. I know where this goes. I get on the plane. And as much as I don't want that to be the end, it has to be. So stop pushing. Please. Because it's hard enough letting go without you holding on to something we can't have."

They'd said everything there was to say. She hadn't left any room for argument or misinterpretation. But when he simply stood, pulled on his jeans and shirt, and left, her heart broke into a thousand pieces. No good-bye. No anything. Just gone.

Leaving her alone in the apartment with a brand new set of rumpled sheets, a maple tree, and a heart she hadn't known could be broken in two short weeks. She stood and turned off his air conditioner, but it didn't eradicate the cold. As immediate silence settled over the apartment, she found odd reassurance in the muffled sounds of the city far below her window.

But they didn't drown the sounds of a broken heart.

Nothing ever would.

She dropped to the bed and curled up with a pillow, breathing his scent, so lost in him that she didn't notice Hell Cat had entered the apartment until he jumped to the bed, probably to chew off her face. A fitting end, she supposed, but he didn't attack—not unless a head butt counted. Instead of unleashing his fangs, he turned in a circle and settled on the bed beside her, his ugly little kitty head tucked near her shoulder.

And purred.

Chapter Fourteen

Crosby extracted a box of hardware from his truck and dropped it on the work bench with enough force to move the piece of furniture several inches across the concrete floor. His dad had pulled him into the office earlier. They were losing money. Fortunately, they had savings from which to draw, but that wouldn't last forever. Probably wouldn't even last months. While he'd been out screwing around with Estelle, his family was taking a hit. Knowing she was leaving made him want to crawl back into his work, but he'd enjoyed every minute he'd spent in the sun. But what had he gained? Nothing. He'd lost money. Lost a piece of himself. Nothing he'd get back…not on either count.

Ethan and Sawyer looked up from their respective places on the other side of the shop.

"What's wrong?" Ethan asked.

"Woman trouble," Sawyer said.

Crosby threw a stray wrench onto the table. It skidded

across the top and tumbled to the floor. "Fuck you."

"No, thank you. Frankly, I've turned down much better offers."

Ethan shot Sawyer a look Crosby couldn't explain, but he damn sure appreciated it. "Get lost," Ethan told his brother.

Sawyer looked back and forth between them and shrugged. "I'll go over the schedule. Maybe Liam and I can cover you this afternoon, Cros."

"Thanks, man." Crosby knew better than to show up in a pissy mood, but he was having a hard time wrapping his head around this thing with Estelle. The worst part was there wasn't anything to work out. They were damned good together, but they belonged on opposite coasts. That was too much of a chasm to close after a couple of weeks.

Ethan dragged a metal folding chair up to the table and sat. "Don't take this the wrong way, but some of us can only wish for the chance you have now."

Jesus Christ. Who invited Dr. Phil? "What is that supposed to mean?"

"Amy," he said. His late wife. "If I had a chance to be with her again, I'd go any damn where she wanted. Siberia, the Antarctic, Easter Island. The Galapagos."

Crosby blew out a breath. "I get it."

"Even fucking California."

"I *get* it." He kicked a chair away from the edge of the table and sat across from his brother—not because he wanted the fucking lecture, but because Ethan didn't mention Amy. Not ever.

Ethan shook his head. "No, you don't. You know how I know you don't? Because you still have your head up your ass."

"You really don't understand." But Crosby was losing some of his fight. Ethan understood more about loss than Crosby ever could, and Crosby respected that.

"I lost my wife, and I can't get her back. Two weeks in, you have a good thing with this woman. You're thirty-one years old, and this is the first time that's ever happened. Ever. You let her walk away, and you'll regret it for the rest of your life."

Crosby leaned back in the chair and met his brother's eyes. It was the first time in a long time Ethan had let the pain show. Or maybe Crosby just hadn't been paying attention. "So what the fuck am I supposed to do, Ethan? I have the business. I can't just walk out—"

"Without you, the business has four completely competent adults to run the show. Five, if you count Sawyer."

"I'm the oldest son."

Ethan glared. "So what? The rest of us still count for something, you asshole."

Crosby choked on something resembling a laugh. "I'm the only one who really connects with this company. You guys will leave, but I'm the one Grandpa trusted to carry on the family legacy."

Ethan didn't smile. "Did Grandpa ever tell you about his plan to see the world?"

"No. He wanted to see the world?"

"Yeah, it was his dream. He was even going to join the Merchant Marines so he could make a living at it."

How had he never known that? Probably because he and Grandpa had usually been talking shop or trading terrible puns. "So what happened? Going from seeing the world to HVAC is kind of a leap."

"He met Grandma. Said that was it for him, that he wasn't going anywhere that would take him away from her. He saw an opportunity with the business and jumped in at the right time, and Fusion was born."

"He gave up his dream?"

"He said he'd never imagined he could fall so hard or love one woman so much. I kind of tuned him out at that point because this hot woman he was talking about was our grandma, but I got the gist. I think he just realized what his dream really was. Maybe you need to do the same thing."

Crosby scrubbed a hand across his face, feeling blindsided. "Why didn't he ever tell me this story?"

"I know you two were close, but—" Ethan's vision clouded over, as if he were staring at something only he could see. "I was trying to get up the nerve to propose, and I talked to him about it. So he told me about the Merchant Marines. I'm sure he would have told you the same story if he were here now. And he'd tell you to drop the family company in a hot minute for this chance."

Crosby frowned. "His dream may have changed, but this is still it. This is what he worked for. I can't tell you how many hours he spent teaching me what he knows. It's a gift. I can't just give it up."

"You're not going to forget what you learned, and nothing will ever take away the time you had together. Seriously man, this thing with Estelle, give it a shot. You say only two weeks, but you're looking at it wrong. Two weeks was long enough for you to know you don't want to let her go. I'm telling you now how lucky you are to have the choice. If you've found someone to love, chase it for all its worth. And if you don't believe we'd all be right here for you if it doesn't work out, then you really are an ass."

With that, his brother turned and headed for the exit. "We'll cover for you this afternoon," he called without looking back. "And we'll cover for you after that if we need to."

Crosby stared at the door for a long while after it closed behind his brother. A couple of weeks was a short time to change his life. But he hadn't needed even that long.

It had happened in a single moment.

He pushed back from the table and found the laptop he kept under the seat of his truck.

It was time to change things all over again.

Estelle almost didn't recognize Grady when he got off the plane. "Are you wearing a grandpa sweater? In *July*?"

"The airplane was cold."

"So you beat up an old man for his sweater?"

Grady laughed. "No, it's my sweater."

"Huh. You know, your sweater doesn't really go with your Star Wars sheets."

"I like my sheets, and I like my sweater." His gray eyes narrowed, and Estelle was struck by how much he favored their father with his dark hair and unusual slate-colored irises. She, meanwhile had her mother's blonde hair and blue eyes. Throw in the fact that Grady towered over her, height-wise, and they didn't look like they had a single gene in common. "Do me a favor," Grady said. "Next time my plane is late, just start drinking without me, wouldya?"

"I'm sorry. I'm…stressed."

"Wanna talk about it?"

"Over lunch," she said as they followed the crowd to the luggage carousel. "How was the conference? Wild?"

"You'd be surprised," he said with practiced indifference. He'd made a cottage industry out of ignoring her every reference to his personal life. "How was the apartment?"

"The air conditioner broke. So did the elevator. And I'm still not sure if I should be afraid of Earl."

Grady laughed. "Yeah, he takes some getting used to. What happened to the air conditioner this time?"

This time? She scowled. "Something involving smoke. You really need to clean your filter more than once a millennium."

"You fixed it?" Grady didn't sound convinced.

"No, I called a repair guy. The company on the fridge."

"They came highly recommended, but I haven't had time to call them. What did you think?"

"That's more of a story for lunch."

Grady's brow hitched to the ceiling.

"Isn't that your bag?"

He turned with just enough time to snatch it off the carousel. *Carousel.* Her heart whimpered. The press of travelers near the baggage area was suffocating, but when she thought about making an escape, the first thing she thought of wasn't home. It was Crosby.

Wrong way, dummy.

She followed a half step behind Grady, allowing him to forge a path through the crowd. By the time they took seats at one of the airport bars, she was exhausted. And thirsty. She ordered a glass of wine.

He asked for a beer, barely looking away from her to do it. Concern etched his face. "So what happened?"

"Are you happy here?" she blurted.

He glanced pointedly at their surroundings. "At the airport?"

"No, genius. In the city." She smiled her thanks as her wine arrived, then downed half the contents of the glass in one swallow.

Grady's eyebrows arched. He watched her, not touching the drink that was set in front of him. "Happier when my apartment hasn't been on fire, but yes, I am."

"Why, though? Why so far from mom and dad?"

He took a long drink before replying. "Is this a trick question?"

"No. It's just…they're not here." She gestured with her arms, nearly hitting a now glaring man who occupied the next stool.

Grady shook his head. "Do you only think of them while you're standing in the cemetery? Or in mom's garden?"

"No, of course not."

"Then who says they're not here? What's going on, Estelle?"

She blinked back the heat of tears, though she wasn't sure for whom. She hadn't cried over her parents in a long time, and Crosby…she just couldn't. Everything had become such a muddled mess. "I met a guy in the grocery store. He turned out to be the HVAC guy, and he's the reason you currently have an air conditioner. They have your old one, by the way, if you want it back. Otherwise you can make monthly payments on a new one."

"Fair enough. Thanks for taking care of that."

"Also, they want to hire you for translating their manuals into English."

"From what language?"

Estelle picked up her wine and took another long swallow. "No, they're in English. Just not plain English. I'm sure when you call, they'll explain better than I ever could."

"And how might I introduce myself? Brother of the girl who met the guy?"

Estelle shifted on the stool "His name is Crosby. I'll spare you the details."

"Don't spare them all. Something must be wrong. You've only taken one dig at my old-man sweater, which, by the way, actually belonged to Dad. That last Christmas before he died, he took me to the airport to catch my flight back to college and gave me this sweater off his back. Told me those tin cans got cold up there so high and to take it to stay warm. I've worn it every flight since."

She blinked back a fresh threat of tears. God, she was an emotional wreck. "I don't remember that sweater on him."

"That's because Mom had just given it to him for Christmas. He wore it out of the house to make her happy, then he sent it a few hundred miles away. He told me he was too young for an old-man sweater. Apparently I wasn't."

Estelle laughed and wiped the unshed moisture from her eyes. "That sounds just like him. And now I feel like a jerk."

Grady waved his hand. "Forget it. What happened with this Crosby? Do I need to go beat him up for you?"

An unladylike snort escaped. "No, but you do need to water a maple tree. It's in your apartment."

Grady looked up from his perusal of the limited menu. "There's a *tree* in my apartment?"

"Yeah."

"Did he screw up that badly?"

"No, he didn't screw up at all. Everything was fantastic. It doesn't feel like two weeks with him, Grady. It feels like forever, in the good way. But we live on opposite coasts. He can't leave the city, and I didn't just earn my master's degree to live in a world dipped in concrete. I can't leave…them."

"Why not?"

"What do you mean, *why not*? What the hell would I do in the city?" Even as she asked, she thought of Crosby's mom and her neighborhood outreach. But she couldn't take money from people who struggled to make ends meet, nor could she earn a living off six linear feet of flower bed at a time. But she could come up with something. She had a ton of equity in her house—more than enough to start over somewhere else. And not just anywhere, but a place where people were moved to tears when they saw their new landscaping. A place that, over the course of two weeks, had actually begun to feel like home. A place with a maple tree that would inevitably meet its demise under the care of her brother.

"I can see the wheels turning, Estelle. Hang out at my place a few more days. Sort it out. I don't think major decisions are supposed to be made in airports."

"Clearly you haven't seen your share of chick flicks. Also, awkward sleeping arrangements at your place."

"I'll sleep on the sofa."

She thought of the moment Crosby tried to stretch out on top of her and flipped the coffee table and its contents. And almost smiled. "Sofa isn't big enough."

Grady closed his eyes for a long moment and shook his head. "First of all, I don't really want to know how or why you came to that conclusion. Secondly, the sofa is a sofa bed."

"Oh." She bit back a smile. "But those things aren't comfortable."

"Which is why I said I'd take it. I've got to say, Estelle, you look about as miserable leaving as you did coming. I got it then, and I deeply appreciate your sacrifice on my behalf. But I don't get it now. You should be twerking your way through the airport, and instead you're moping over a half-full glass of wine."

She glanced quickly to either side, praying no one heard him. Satisfied she would keep her mortification to herself, she turned to him with a lowered voice. "I absolutely do not twerk for any reason. I don't even know why you know that word, but that aside, this is an awkward conversation to have with your brother."

"Yeah, well, I don't have a brother, so spill."

She buried her face in her hands and wiped her eyes. "I cannot begin to explain this without sounding like a stupid thirteen-year-old girl drawing hearts in my notebook. Crosby and I just connected in a way I've never connected with anyone before. Three months into any other relationship, if I felt like this I'd start whispering *he's the one* to my girlfriends over empty wine bottles."

"But?"

She shrugged. "But it hasn't been three months. I've known him thirteen days."

He narrowed his eyes. "You do realize thirteen days won't lead to three months if you leave."

"What about mom?" Emotion welled in her throat, threatening the last shreds of her composure. If Grady told her their mother didn't matter, he'd find himself wearing what was left of her wine.

He tugged at the neck of his old man sweater, leaving her to wonder if the loss still choked him as it did her. "She created that garden for everyone to enjoy," he said. "It was never intended to chain you down. She wants you to be happy. She'd probably really love it if you were here making me miserable."

"That's an excellent point." And one with which she couldn't argue.

"And doesn't that garden have about a thousand volunteers?"

"Maybe a hundred," she admitted.

"I know the garden is important to you, but don't sacrifice people for things. You and mom and dad have made a difference there. Maybe it's time to move on. Spread the joy a little."

Estelle hiked her bag onto her shoulder and jumped down from her stool. "You're right."

"I am?"

"Yep." She threw a twenty on the bar, abandoning the remains of her wine, and headed back in the direction of the taxi stand, her brother scrambling to follow.

"Should I be worried?" he asked as he maneuvered after her. Her legs were no match for his long strides, and he closed the distance easily.

She was about to answer when she ran head-first into a man. One she'd know anywhere. She took a step back as his bright green eyes settled over her, then her focus shifted to the paper he held in his hand.

It was a boarding pass.

Flight 185.

Hers.

Chapter Fifteen

Estelle's stunned blue eyes were brighter than ever. "What are you doing here?"

He couldn't get a read on her, dammit. That, and she was with a tall, vaguely familiar guy who might be her brother but looked *nothing* like her.

Her gaze tracked back and forth between the men. "Crosby, this is my brother Grady."

Grady's brow lifted just enough to suggest he'd heard the story. Crosby just wished he knew which version. "Nice to meet you," he said, offering his hand.

"Likewise. And I'm sure I'll see you again, so let me slink off and leave you to this moment, whatever it is."

Estelle elbowed her brother in the stomach.

Grady rolled his eyes. "I won't wait up."

"He's going to kill my tree, you know. Maybe you should reclaim it for your mother's yard."

"I'll get right on that," he muttered, still a little unsure what was going on. Estelle was headed away from her plane, not to it. Although it was early enough. Maybe she was just walking her brother out, only it was more like she charged full steam ahead while Grady trailed after her, his face a mask of concern and bewilderment.

Estelle's blue eyes narrowed. "After you fly to California?"

He looked at the boarding pass he'd forgotten he held. So much for the surprise, although he wasn't sure it would be a good one.

"I have a plan," he said.

"Does your plan involve a fire escape?" she asked.

Relief flooded him. Any mention of the fire escape had to be good. "See? There are definite perks to the city."

"Then why are you leaving it?"

"Ah, that. I've done a little research. Turns out we've tapped our market here, so I'm heading up a move to the suburbs."

Her brow raised. "You're moving Fusion to the suburbs?"

"Not moving—we'll keep the business here as well—but expanding. And not *the* suburbs, but *yours*. Or, rather, your town.

Estelle stared. "No."

"No?" He blinked, a bit taken aback. He'd half expected she really might be done with him, but standing there like an island in the flood of people brushing past had given him hope.

"Expanding to the suburbs might be a great idea," she said, "but expand to your own. Stay near the core of your business."

Dammit. His father had said the same thing before reluctantly agreeing. But once he'd done so, he'd thrown his full support behind the plan, or at least a more thorough exploration thereof.

"No yourself," he said. "The chance to get to know you better is worth the risk. Unless you don't want that chance."

"I do," she said. "That's why I'm staying."

He blinked, unsure he'd heard her correctly. "You're *staying*?"

"I'm staying. Turns out there's a fifth thing I love about the city," she said. "You."

His heart hammered. The words refused to sink in. "You...*me*?"

Estelle laughed, albeit weakly. "That must be your inner cave man speaking," she said. "My best friend is here and my brother and...those are just excuses to be with you. My brother said I could stay with him. He offered to take the sofa." His face must have twisted because she laughed. "It's a fold out."

Someone seriously needed to teach him how to do a cartwheel. "I have a better idea. What if your brother keeps his bed and you share mine? If you're moving a few thousand miles to be near me, I'll be damned if I'll let you stop on the wrong floor of the apartment building."

"Are you sure?"

"Are you kidding me? I've thought of little else. And I have a fire escape outside my window, too, you know."

A thousand people rushed by, but he only saw her. Her eyes were watery and bright. He hoped that was a good thing. "I'd love to see your fire escape," she said with a laugh. "And on a *totally* different subject, I'd like to work with your mother," she said. "Not just flower beds, though. Gardens— maybe community plots where we'll grow vegetables for neighbors to share."

"My mother would love that," he said. And that was an understatement. His mother *loved* Estelle. His whole family had. "What about you, though? Is that going to keep you happy? What about your mother's garden?"

Estelle gave a slight, conspiratorial grin. "Don't you ever tell my brother I said this, but he just made a lot of sense. There are people there to care for that garden. There are people *here* to care for me."

"Damn straight."

She tilted her head and hugged her arms across her chest. Her eyes danced. "I wasn't going to get on the plane, but since you're here, why don't you go home with me? I'll show you the garden, and if we're still speaking after a few days, we'll fly back here together. If you have time to stay a while, I mean."

Relief flooded him. He hadn't felt that damn happy since…well, the fire escape. Her words filled an unfathomable void. Hell yeah, he had time. "I have all the time in the world for you."

"I do have to warn you about one thing," she said.

"What's that?"

"No fire escapes. Not anywhere."

"That's okay," he said. "I'll build one just for you. *Anywhere*."

Epilogue

The Friday night crowd packed Foam's For You, a neighborhood bar frequented by the Chase brothers, along
with what had to be half the borough. Estelle sipped her
Long Island Iced Tea through the stir straw and sat back
in the booth, sandwiched between Crosby and her brother.
Liam and Ethan sat across from them, as had Sawyer until
he saw one of his ex-hookups across the room.

"She doesn't stand a chance," Liam said, shaking his
head.

"It's the Chase charm," Ethan said. He raised his nearly
empty frosted mug in a mock toast and quickly lost it to a
passing waitress.

"Be right back with this, hon," she called over her shoulder.

Ethan shrugged. "Can't beat the service."

Estelle sat back in the crook of Crosby's arm and rested
her hand on his thigh. He felt good. He felt *incredible*, and
the jolt that shot through her whenever she thought of him

or touched him or was touched *by* him may have become familiar in the weeks since they flew together to the left coast, but it was no less thrilling. If anything, it was more so.

When they'd returned to California, she'd had a long talk with her difficult client and had sold her, mostly, on a more reasonable plan. She'd have to see that job out personally, but the rest would be easily handed over to someone else. She had also talked to a realtor about selling her house. The realtor confirmed Estelle's equity was more than enough for her to start over. Even better, she'd known just the person to take over the memorial garden on Estelle's behalf. Crosby was still running numbers on the business expansion, and she still had to fly back to the west coast a handful of times to finish out a couple of seasonal jobs, but it was a small sacrifice for everything she gained. Even the city had begun to feel like home, though she'd never admit it in front of Crosby's brothers. Or hers.

The last thing Grady needed to hear was any version of *you were right*.

Even if he had been.

Even if he damn well knew it.

She smiled up at Crosby, who turned his head so his lips grazed her ear. "I love you."

Fire peppered her veins every time he said those words, and every time she said them back. "I love you more."

"Oh, God," Ethan said. "If you two have this *argument* one more time."

Liam nudged him. "Hey, pool table is opening up."

"Thank you," Ethan said. He jumped from the booth and waited for Liam to follow. "Winner pays for the night," Ethan said with a smirk.

"You're damn…wait a minute."

Whatever Ethan responded was lost to the noise. Crosby shook his head and laughed as Grady moved across the table from them. "You two *are* pretty disgusting," he said.

"You sure you want to put up with us?" Crosby asked.

"Ha. I'm stuck with my sister anyway." He took a swallow of his drink and grinned. "As for the job, you forget I mostly work alone. In my apartment. Which apparently I was allergic to upon my return."

"Was it the tree?" she asked, feigning innocence.

Grady rolled his eyes. "Only if it grows fur."

Estelle gave up the fight not to laugh. "Okay, there was a cat."

"It bit me on the ass," Crosby said. "I tried to get her to look, but she wouldn't."

Estelle elbowed him. "You *so* would not let me look."

"I can only assume you looked," Grady said warily. "At which point you raided my nightstand."

Estelle gave Crosby a pointed look, then addressed Grady. "They were there because you make balloon animals, right?"

Crosby shook his head knowingly. "I told her they were absolutely not there to make balloon animals."

"Well, you don't think he was sleeping with anyone on *those* sheets do you?"

"Oh, God, Estelle. You're my sister. Could you *stop*?"

"You need to ask Sawyer what his secret is. You need a woman."

"As evidenced by the empty box of…balloon animals?" Grady asked.

"Hey," she protested. "We replaced them."

"Actually, I think we used them again. And I think it was more than half empty," Crosby supplied. "Because—"

Grady lifted his drink as if to hide behind it. "No offense, man, but there are some things a guy just doesn't want to know about his sister."

Crosby grinned. "Like what she did with your Star Wars sheets?"

Grady set his drink down with a solid *thunk*. "You mean she didn't throw them out?"

"Nu—*oomph*." Estelle buried her elbow in Crosby's side, cutting him off.

"I want my sheets," Grady said.

"Are you kidding me? I can't even believe they make those in queen size."

"Estelle, for the love of God, my balloon animals don't care what my sheets look like."

Crosby snickered.

She rolled her eyes. "Fine. You can have your sheets back, but I'm going to find you a woman. Maybe Sawyer can give you dating tips."

Crosby raised his hand. "Let me just interject here and say Sawyer's idea of dating involves…not dating. His so-called relationships are over when the sun rises."

"A string of meaningless encounters," Estelle supplied. "Do you think he's lonely?"

"I'm not going to ponder his motivation. I just wish he'd stop trying so hard. It's like he goes out of his way to find women who want nothing of a relationship, and he's no better than they are."

Estelle narrowed her eyes. "And your last relationship was *when*?"

Crosby shrugged. "Not relevant. I recognize self-destruction when I see it. He prides himself on his playboy reputation. He doesn't seem to think there's a negative connotation there."

"Then we'll just have to show him he's wrong," Estelle said. I think it's the least we can do after he spilled the pickle incident to your parents."

Grady drained his frosted mug. "Can I just say how grateful I am that Estelle has someone else to nag?"

"You're welcome," Crosby said.

Grady snorted. "I might need that in writing."

Crosby laughed. "Not a chance."

Estelle's phone dinged. She pulled up the message. "I got an offer on my house," she said. "Full price."

Crosby looked at her like she'd hung the moon, sending her into a pit of warm and fuzzy. "So we're doing this?"

Her heart soared. Not an ending, but a beginning. "We're doing this."

He leaned close and whispered in her ear. "On the fire escape?"

She laughed. "Every chance we get."

Acknowledgments

Tracy, I should build a shrine to you. One made of coffee or vodka. Or maybe both. You rock so hard, and the day you were gifted to me was one of the best ever. I appreciate your patience and your time in ways you can't possible know. When the day comes that you finally get to throw something at me, I promise not to duck.

Heather, you *OMG spoke to me*, and now you're human. A human who skewers with a red and white barber-striped phallus, but that just makes you that much cooler. You've given me some of the most amazing compliments and bits of encouragement of my writing life, so I hope you don't find it the least bit creepy that I tend to bask in them from time to time. (This is, of course, considerably more productive than throwing my computer against a wall.)

Michelle, I seriously *need* you in my life. All 100+ of our daily emails are as necessary as breathing. I don't know what I'd do without your support, friendship, and shared insanity, but I'm sure whatever it is would make the evening news.

And, as always, throughout this process, my family hasn't killed me nor I them. I knew they were awesome, but this proves it.

About the Author

Sarah and her husband of what he calls "many long, long years" live on the mid-Atlantic coast with their six young children, all of whom are perfectly adorable when they're asleep. She never dreamed of becoming an author, but as a homeschooling mom, she often jokes she writes fiction because if she wants anyone to listen to her, she has to make them up. (As it turns out, her characters aren't much better than the kids). When not buried under piles of laundry, she may be found adrift in the Atlantic (preferably on a boat) or seeking that ever-elusive perfect writing spot where not even the kids can find her.

She loves creating unforgettable stories while putting her characters through an unkind amount of torture—a hobby that has nothing to do with living with six children. (Really.) Though she adores sexy contemporary romance, Sarah writes in many genres including historical and ghostly supernatural romance and romantic suspense. Her ever-growing roster of releases may be found on Amazon, Barnes & Noble, Kobo, iBooks, Google Books, and Entangled Publishing.

Also by Sarah Ballance...

THE MARRIAGE AGENDA

RUBY HILL

Discover historical romance by Sarah Ballance

HER WICKED SIN

AN UNEXPECTED SIN

THE SINS OF A FEW

www.ingramcontent.com/pod-product-compliance
Lightning Source LLC
Chambersburg PA
CBHW050820180626
46814CB00004B/1387